FALSE PRETENCES

When Ginger Maddox, a San Francisco stock-broker, meets handsome Neil Cameron, she becomes attracted to him. But then mysterious things begin to happen, involving Neil's aunts. After a romantic weekend with Neil, Ginger overhears a telephone conversation confirming her growing suspicions that he's involved in illegal trading. She's devastated, fearing that this could end their relationship. But it's the elderly aunts who help show the young people that love will find a way.

PHYLLIS HUMPHREY

FALSE PRETENCES

Complete and Unabridged

LINFORD
Leicester

First published in 2006
in the United States of America

First Linford Edition
published 2009

British Library CIP Data

Humphrey, Phyllis A.
False pretences
- - (Linford romance library)
1. Women stockbrokers- -California
- -San Francisco- -Fiction. 2. Love stories.
3. Large type books.
I. Title II. Series
813.6–dc22

ISBN 978–1–84782–756–2

11228483 ⊆

Published by
F. A. Thorpe (Publishing)
Anstey, Leicestershire

Set by Words & Graphics Ltd.
Anstey, Leicestershire
Printed and bound in Great Britain by
T. J. International Ltd., Padstow, Cornwall

This book is printed on acid-free paper

To my husband, Curt,
Whom I also met in San Francisco

My thanks to the fourteen ladies who helped me to start our investment club, Tuesday Traders, and whose support and encouragement enabled me to write *Wall Street On $20 A Month*, as well as this novel.

1

On a scale of one to ten, Ginger decided her office at Benson, Field and Smith, Stock Brokers, was about a four. No walls, just partitions to mark the cubicles. A desk, two chairs, computer and telephone: she didn't really need more. She needed another client or two, but she felt that this was the right occupation for her and, if she worked hard, more clients would show up soon. She bent over the list of possibles on her desk and was about to pick up the phone and call one when a deep, masculine voice greeted her.

'Good morning.'

Ginger raised her head and her gaze met the deep brown eyes of a man standing in her doorway. He was tall and well built, with hair a darker shade of red than hers, and he wore a handsome Burberry raincoat. She couldn't help smiling. The man must be a stranger; native San Franciscans seldom wore raincoats in June, The morning fog would soon burn off, no matter how gloomy it seemed at the moment.

'May I help you?'

'I'm looking for a stockbroker,' he said, with a slight shrug of his broad shoulders. 'The receptionist mentioned a Mr. Maddox and pointed me in this direction.'

'It's Ginger Maddox,' she said. 'And you're in the right place; I am a registered representative.' Her husband Colin had worked there before her, and — when he was fatally struck by a car — she'd been persuaded to take his place.

The stranger stood, unmoving, in her doorway, and she saw that he was not only over six feet tall, but good-looking, with an aristocratic nose and full lips set in a squarish sun-tanned face. Ginger couldn't help wondering how a redhead could tan so well; it had never been possible for her.

'I was expecting — ' he began, and then paused.

'You were expecting a man,' Ginger finished for him. 'As you know, there are many women representatives these days. And besides,' she added, with a broad smile, hoping to convince him to stay, for she desperately needed more clients, 'it's my turn.'

'I beg your pardon?' He came forward, filling the small space with his imposing presence.

'Please sit down.' Ginger pointed to the walnut arm chair. 'The receptionist sent you to me because each one is called in turn when a new client comes into the office.'

He continued to stand, so Ginger was forced to rise as well, although at five feet nine in her heels, she still found it necessary to look up to him.

'I see,' he answered, then repeated, 'It's your turn.' He paused. 'I don't mean to appear chauvinistic, but I had

3

been expecting a man, and — ' He broke off.

At least he had the decency to be embarrassed about his sexist remarks.

'I assure you I'm perfectly capable,' she said. 'Women take the same course of study for these positions as men, and must turn in equally high marks.'

'It's not that,' then added, 'you're so young.'

'Thank you for the compliment, but I'm almost thirty.' She had just turned twenty-eight, but had already learned that people in their thirties and forties — she judged this man to be somewhere between — had difficulty accepting investment advice from someone too much their junior. And she hadn't lied; twenty-eight was a lot closer to thirty than it was to twenty.

'Please be seated,' she said again, but he only stared at her until she could feel a flush rising to her usually fair skin, and then he said, 'Excuse me,' turned and left.

She watched him return to the

4

receptionist for a moment, then proceed in the direction of the manager's office. Her pulse pounded. What was he saying to her boss? She almost trembled with outrage. How could he do that without even giving her a chance?

She sank down abruptly in her chair and turned her attention to the list of names on the desk; but the words blurred before her eyes, and her mind refused to concentrate. All she could think of was the man in the manager's office, no doubt discussing her.

Jim Blake, the manager of this branch, was more than her employer; he was her friend as well. After his divorce a few years before, she and her husband Colin had sometimes invited Jim to dinner, and had also sailed with him and other friends on his twenty-eight-foot boat in San Francisco Bay. Jim was fifteen years older than Ginger and had taken an almost fatherly interest in her when Colin had been killed in the automobile accident. Since she was between jobs at the time, he had urged her to enter the firm.

Still, friends or not, she was not a charity case and would never let him down. She had thrown herself into studying the market and found that she not only liked the world of buying and selling securities, but apparently had an aptitude for it. Once she acquired a long list of satisfied customers and generated high commissions for the firm, Jim would see his decision justified and be proud of her. Certainly, if hard work was any criterion for success, she would attain that goal before she reached the age of the insensitive man who had just left her office.

As if responding to her unspoken thoughts, the man himself once more appeared in her doorway. Her eyes widened. What had Jim said to him?

'Ms. Maddox, please forgive my earlier rudeness.' He removed his coat, placed it carelessly across the back of the chair, and sat down.

Ginger didn't answer, she was too

surprised. Plus, his earlier dismissal remained fresh in her mind.

'You must have thought my remarks were based on your being a woman. That wasn't the case at all. It was a misunderstanding. Mr. Blake told me how qualified you are, a graduate of Stanford and a member of Mensa. I'm very impressed.'

Her hurt dissolved slowly with his compliments. She felt some gratitude for his changed attitude, and he looked and sounded sincere. 'Thank you. It was kind of Mr. Blake to give me such a flattering recommendation.'

'And then,' he continued, 'there are my aunts. They live in the city and apparently worked with your late husband, Colin Maddox. They told me I must look him up for my own investment needs.'

Ginger's heart plummeted. So she was not being chosen for her expertise after all, but because the man's relatives were satisfied with Colin's performance.

Again, hiding her feelings, she remained calm. 'What are your aunts' names?'

'Mary and Carrie Dillon.'

Ginger reached for her client book and scanned the list. 'I contacted them, but they never returned my calls.'

'Perhaps they didn't recognize the name. They're elderly ladies and sometimes a little — ' After a pause he said, 'They may not have made the connection.'

'But the fact is,' Ginger said, 'I am not my husband. Perhaps, now that you know your aunts' recommendation was not for me at all, you prefer to see someone else.'

As soon as she spoke, she regretted the words. As badly as she needed new clients, why this reluctance, why encourage him to try someone else? Did it have anything to do with his charming smile and her quickening heartbeat?

He studied her face before answering. 'Had that been the case, I wouldn't have returned to you. But here I am.'

Ginger found his gaze unnerving and his velvet brown eyes seemed to bore into her. She looked away, tried to cover the confusion of her conflicting emotions. Taking a deep breath, she reached into her desk drawer for a new client form to fill out and plunged ahead. 'Very well, I'm certain we can work well together in the future, Mr. Dillon.'

'I'm sure we can. And the name is Cameron,' he said. 'My aunts' names are Dillon, but mine is Cameron.' He paused. 'I should have made that clear at the outset. They're my mother's sisters, and never married.' His gaze swept over her face. 'In spite of my earlier reluctance, I see now that this could be a very rewarding experience.'

Ginger's gaze flew to him once more. What did he mean by that? Was he hinting at a different kind of relationship? Unfortunately, since Colin's death, she'd run into too many men who wanted more from her than market opinions. She put her sudden doubts behind her. Mr. —

'Your first name?' she asked, pen poised over the form.

'MacKenzie,' he said.

'Middle name or initial?'

'Neil.'

Ginger had always liked that name, thought she'd give it to a son if she ever had one. She relaxed. Mr. Cameron seemed business-like, just the sort of client she wanted. 'Will there be any other names on the account?'

'No, I've just moved to San Francisco and I'm single.'

So he was apparently unmarried. For a second the news pleased her; then she told herself it was irrelevant. Once the form was filled out, she began her usual questions for clients. 'What are your investment objectives, Mr. Cameron?'

'Capital appreciation,' he said. 'I have no need for present income. As a matter of fact, I prefer not to have large dividends which may be taxable.'

'Are you interested in municipals?'

'Definitely not. Bonds of any kind are far too tame.' His look turned from serious to smiling, and his brown eyes seemed to twinkle with mischief. 'I'm looking for growth and willing to be a little aggressive.'

She liked his smile. She had already forgiven him for his earlier chauvinism. 'A shade speculative, perhaps?'

'Yes, I don't mind taking a flyer now and then into a new company that might turn out to be another Microsoft. In fact, I discussed that with your manager. He assured me you wouldn't be too conservative for my needs.'

'I hope that's true.' She remembered how her mother often lamented having a red-haired child, impetuous and inquisitive from her earliest years.

'Do you want to purchase some stock now, or do you prefer to give me a day or two to prepare some recommendations for you?'

'Both, I think,' he said. 'Do you have something to recommend at this time?'

'As a matter of fact, I do have a very interesting possibility. It's called Taylor Technology; it went public only two years ago.' She suddenly realized he was frowning. 'Is something the matter?'

'That's the electronics firm in what you Californians call Silicon Valley, isn't it? Forget them.' His manner was abrupt and Ginger felt her earlier hostility returning.

'I beg your pardon,' she said. 'I've investigated the company and it's not one of those dot.com startups that — '

'I'm sorry,' he interrupted, 'but I happen to know that stock isn't going anywhere.'

Ginger was taken aback, but managed to speak softly. 'It's your decision of course. But our research department did a very thorough study recently and I visited their offices not two weeks ago for a first-hand look.'

His face softened, he smiled again, and she took advantage of his changed attitude.

'I predict,' she said, 'that their next quarter's earnings will be fifty percent higher and at a price/earnings ratio of only fifteen.'

'Well, perhaps I should take a chance, especially since you guarantee it's a good deal.'

'Guarantee? Mr. Cameron, you know there are no guarantees in the stock market.'

'But you were so positive about it a moment ago. Are you revising your opinion? Why?'

She raised her chin and straightened her back. 'Very well, Mr. Cameron, buy some shares in this company and, if they haven't increased in value within six months, I'll repay your brokerage commissions personally.'

Her words seemed to come from some other person, and their rashness only began to penetrate after they left her lips. What had made her say such a thing?

The room became ominously quiet and she regretted her outburst. Besides being drop-dead handsome, what was there about this man that made her behave so strangely?

He took her hand in his. 'You have a

13

deal, Ms. — See here, I can't call you Ms. Maddox. We're going to be very close from now on. I'll call you Ginger instead. And you must call me Mac; everybody does.'

His strong hand dwarfed hers. It was hard and smooth. Its touch sent disturbing sensations through her, and she pulled away as soon as she could do it politely. She swiveled her chair around to face the small computer terminal in the corner and tapped in the stock symbol of Taylor Technology. Its current price flashed on the screen.

'Twenty-nine and a half,' she quoted, using every ounce of her strength to remain riveted on the transaction. 'How many shares would you like?'

'Whatever a hundred thousand will buy,' he said.

A volcano erupted in Ginger's chest. One hundred thousand dollars! Why the commission on that was — was — staggering!

Once more, her mouth open in surprise, she stared at Cameron and could say nothing.

'Are there enough shares outstanding?' he asked, his eyebrows arched inquisitively. 'Or is it a thin stock?'

'No, no,' she murmured, heart pounding, her face feeling hot and as red as her hair. 'I mean, yes,' she stammered. She'd almost memorized the statistics earlier but now she hardly knew what she was saying.

'Good.' He stood up and flung his coat over his arm in a careless gesture. 'It's been a pleasure meeting you. I have no permanent daytime telephone yet, but you can reach me in the evenings at the number I gave you.'

She had risen when he did, and now she said goodbye in a barely audible whisper.

He thrust his hand forward and she took it automatically, its firm touch reminding her of both her rashness and of the sudden physical attraction he held for her. He released her, turned and left, and she watched him walk through the office. He paused to look up at the electronic stock board with its moving letters and numbers, then he sailed through the doors and disappeared into the crowds on Montgomery Street.

Ginger stood still for several more seconds, still flustered. Then she caught a glimpse of Jim Blake re-entering his office and remembered what Cameron had hinted. The temper that went with her red hair flared again. Token woman, was she? Well, she'd show Jim; she'd be the best representative that ever sat in this office.

As for Mr. Cameron and his guarantees, she'd show him too.

* * *

MacKenzie Neil Cameron hailed a cab, told the driver his destination, and thought about the woman he had just met. There was only one word for her: a knockout. Perfect features, a great figure, and that short curly hair that made a coppery halo around her face.

He'd convinced himself he preferred women with long blonde hair, certainly not a redhead like himself. He'd always hated his own hair when he was a child, hating being called, 'Red' or 'Carrot-top.' Fortunately, he'd been able to joke about it himself and then grew tall enough that even such mild bullying stopped. But Ginger Maddox —

Talk about mixing business with pleasure. What a pleasure it was going to be to handle this assignment. Of course, his business came first and — depending on what Ms. Maddox knew and when she knew it — she might not appreciate his interest in her at all. Still, he had a job to do; and he'd keep his word about that, no matter what the cost.

2

In spite of the many telephone calls she made for the rest of the morning, Ginger found Mr. Cameron intruded far too frequently on her thoughts. Was it merely because she had made the rash promise to return his commissions if Taylor Technology failed to rise in price over the next six months; or because he was one of the handsomest men she had ever seen, with a magnetism that caused sensations she had not experienced in years?

Or, perhaps it was the circumstances of their meeting and the mysterious aunts he had mentioned who had once worked with Colin. Odd that she didn't remember Colin ever saying anything about the ladies.

She reached into her file drawer and pulled out the folder marked 'Dillon,' grateful again that Jim Blake had turned over so many of Colin's clients to her. Whether he had hired her out of pity, or to be the 'token woman' in his office, one fact was certainly clear: he had done his utmost to help her get started. Of course, not every one of Colin's clients had been referred to her. Some had very active accounts and they had been turned over to other representatives in the firm. It had, after all, been more than a year since Colin's death; one couldn't expect customers to wait that long for someone to service their accounts, even if they were willing to switch to their previous broker's widow.

The Dillon file was thin — it had not been a very active account, she saw — very few transactions, all of them 'buy' orders. Perhaps this was why Colin had never mentioned the ladies. And yet, they were apparently so impressed with him that they had urged their nephew to look him up. Still, elderly maiden ladies didn't have to be particularly logical, she supposed. She shrugged, returned the file to the drawer and glanced at her watch.

The New York Stock Exchange would close in five minutes, and then she could leave the building, have her lunch, and see about purchasing a new dress.

A shadow appeared between her and the light and, looking up, she saw Jim Blake standing in her doorway.

'Come in, Jim.'

He dropped his plump figure into her extra chair and ran his fingers through his thick salt and pepper hair. 'How's it going today, Ginger?'

'That's an innocent question,' she teased him. 'It's quite obvious you're curious to know what happened with Mr. Cameron.'

'Well,' he admitted, 'I'm naturally interested. The man appeared somewhat irate when he reached my desk. I thought at first you had been rude to him.'

'Rude?' Ginger almost exploded the word.

'Calm down,' Jim soothed. 'I soon

learned better. He was looking for Colin, and the girl at the desk just caught the name 'Maddox' and directed him to you. He was surprised to find a woman instead of a man. I also detected a certain — shall we say — 'bias' in his outlook.'

'Bias is putting it nicely,' Ginger said. 'And I must thank you for what were apparently a lot of good recommendations on my behalf.'

'It was nothing but the truth,' Jim continued. 'You are a very bright lady and I'm proud of your achievements.'

'Thanks again, but I wish I could reward your confidence with more clients than I've been able to produce so far.'

'Give yourself time; you've only been here four months. Rome wasn't built in a day, you know.'

Ginger laughed. 'What a clever saying; I must remember that.'

Jim laughed with her. 'I'm serious though,' he added. 'Even Colin wasn't bringing in a decent commission check for the first year, as you, of all people, ought to remember.'

'That's true.'

'Be patient. Relax and do the best you can. By the way,' he added, after a pause, 'you did land Cameron didn't you?'

Ginger laughed lightly again. 'Yes, I did, thanks in no small part to you.' Her thoughts flew back to her rash promise to the man they were discussing, but she decided not to tell Jim about that, at least not yet. 'It may not have been my expertise, however, but your very kind remarks, along with a strong recommendation from his two maiden aunts.'

'Maiden aunts? That's a new one. By the way, you are coming to my housewarming Saturday, aren't you?'

'Yes, in fact I'm actually going to buy a new dress for the occasion.'

'I'm flattered.'

She remembered the last new dress she'd bought, over two years before, for a formal party with Colin. She pushed the memory back into a deep recess. 'I want to see your new townhouse.'

The ringing of the telephone interrupted them, and Ginger excused herself and picked up the instrument.

'Miss Mary Dillon on line five,' the operator said.

Eyes widening, Ginger looked across at Jim, then covered the mouthpiece with her free hand, and whispered to her boss, 'Speak of the — angels, one of Mr. Cameron's maiden aunts is on the phone right now.'

Jim made a circle with his thumb and forefinger and left her office, and Ginger went back to the telephone. 'Put her through.'

* * *

Half an hour later, Ginger was not shopping, as she had expected. Instead she stood in the lobby of the Greenhouse Restaurant, eagerly scanning every woman who entered. Soon two short, doll-like ladies wearing identical

23

coats, identical small hats perched on identically coiffed grey hair, and with identical bright blue eyes in identical faces, approached her. They were twins in every sense of the word.

The one on the left spoke first. 'Mrs. Maddox, I believe. I'm Mary Dillon. This is my sister — '

'Carrie Dillon,' said the lady on the right. 'We're very glad to meet you. Our nephew did an excellent job of — '

' — describing you,' finished Mary Dillon. 'Shall we be seated? We don't usually wait this long for — '

' — our lunch,' Carrie concluded.

Her gaze bouncing back and forth between the two ladies, Ginger was almost too surprised to speak. They couldn't have resembled Cameron less, being as petite as he was tall, with almost pure white hair, whereas his was deep, mahogany red, and with piercing blue eyes, where his were soft and brown. True, they were all good-looking people. Perhaps there was a hint of the beauty that once may have belonged to

the ladies in Cameron's even, handsome features; and, now that she
thought of it, their mouths were shaped
somewhat alike, although the ladies' were
definitely more feminine. Age — she
guessed them to be in their seventies
— had not pinched their faces and thinned
their lips to tight lines. In fact, Ginger
was surprised to see that their skin was
quite smooth and unwrinkled.

The waitress appeared at that moment
and led them into the restaurant. The
sun shone through the whitewashed
greenhouse ceiling of the main room,
casting a pale warm glow on the white
bamboo kiosks, the curved-back chairs
with their colorful cotton print cushions
and on the almost jungle-like profusion
of tropical plants everywhere. The
square table they were offered had a
sparkling glass top under colorful place
mats, matching napkins, and red
anthuriums in a white vase. The menus
were placed open before them, they
studied the choices and gave their
order.

'Well,' Mary said, smiling broadly at Ginger. 'It's time we got better acquainted. I'm sorry it's taken us — '

' — so long to get around to that,' Carrie added. 'We were informed of your husband's death and that you were handling the account, and ought to have — '

' — called you at once to express our sympathy.'

Ginger swiveled her head back and forth between the two ladies as they spoke, slightly confused. Did they always finish one another's sentences that way? And how would she ever tell them apart? She couldn't go through life expecting Mary always to be on her left and Carrie her right to know which was which.

'Our nephew — we call him Neil — told us,' Mary said, 'that you are a remarkably beautiful young lady, and we must say — '

' — he was right,' Carrie concluded. 'He's never been partial to red-heads before, hated his own hair color when he was a boy, you know — '

' — but I think that was probably his reason — '

' — but I don't think that's important now,' Carrie said, interrupting her sister. 'Let's get on with — '

' — our mission? Very well. About our securities — '

For the next hour Ginger continued to turn first to one lady and then the other, hardly getting a word in the conversation herself, as the two women told her about their investments. So far as she could make out, Cameron knew very little about his aunts' private business. As their only living relative, he was their heir, and they didn't consider it proper that he learn their true worth. Not that he was in any way eager to do so.

'Heavens no,' Miss Carrie said. 'The boy hasn't a greedy bone in his body. In fact, how he managed to accumulate so much himself — '

' — when he had no interest in business or finance as a student, has always been a wonder to us.'

Their reluctance to discuss it with him stemmed, instead, from their upbringing, when nice people did not discuss things as crass as money. Nevertheless, the ladies took a kind of impish delight in putting theirs to unusual uses; and it amazed Ginger to hear their stories of how they had once owned a racehorse, an oil well and part of a prize fighter.

'In our younger days that was,' Mary said, 'when we were only seventy.'

'We're eight-five now,' Carrie added, 'and only fit for tame things — '

' — like the stock market,' Mary finished.

Tame or not, their idea of investing in the stock market was certainly unique, and Ginger was intrigued by the ladies and how they handled their money. As she wondered why Colin had never mentioned them, they solved the riddle.

'We didn't know your late husband very well. We gave him only a few very small orders — '

' — just to test him, you see. And then, when we were sure he was the soul of discretion, he — '

' — had that unfortunate accident. But Neil says — '

' — that you are a person to be trusted completely, and now that we see you, we understand — '

Ginger didn't know how MacKenzie, or rather Neil, Cameron could possibly have made such an assessment of her in such a brief time as their conversation in her office had taken. Still, there had been that occasional odd look on his face as he studied her. What quality had he looked for — and apparently found — that he had called his aunts at once and told them to contact her?

'But you see,' Carrie went on, 'you must never tell him anything at all about what we buy and sell. You will keep this in strictest confidence — '

' — like a doctor or lawyer — '

'Naturally,' Ginger answered.

'That's why we didn't want to meet in your office,' Mary said. 'We'd like all

29

of our discussions to be handled as discreetly as possible. No one must know what we're doing.'

'I understand.' Nevertheless, Ginger couldn't help wondering just what kind of transactions they wanted her to handle. Like their nephew before them, they were making it sound quite mysterious. So far, the things they had mentioned were speculative — but far from dangerous — except for First Continental, which was an insurance company and a very conservative choice. At any rate, they so obviously had their minds made up, and had not asked Ginger for advice, that it would have been both rude and unethical for her to suggest they didn't know what they were doing with their own money.

'We'd like a thousand shares of First Continental,' Carrie said.

Ginger nodded; that was a fine, conservative investment.

But Mary's next words shocked her. 'And will you please purchase a thousand shares of Taylor Technology for us — '

' — at the market tomorrow,' Carrie added.

Ginger stopped writing in her notebook and looked up at them. 'Are you sure? Taylor Technology?' Their nephew had obviously suggested the stock to them, but while it was all right for him — since he had suggested he wanted to invest in that type of stock — surely they were too old to do the same thing.

'Are you aware it's a biotechnology company? That's a rather speculative investment for — ' Then she stopped herself. Didn't considering the age of the sisters as a basis for recommendations smack of ageism, discrimination? On the other hand, diligence required she inform her clients when she thought they were choosing inappropriate stocks.

'Yes,' Carrie repeated, 'Taylor Technology. We know all about what they do. We like being on the cutting edge. And now we'll be going.'

While Ginger was still thinking about the modern phrase Carrie had used, they rose from their chairs in unison, and Mary picked up the check that had just been deposited on the edge of the table.

'Please allow me,' Ginger said, reaching for it.

'We wouldn't hear of it,' Carrie answered. 'You were our guest.'

Still protesting mildly, Ginger followed the ladies back to the entrance lobby, where Mary dropped the check on the counter and said to the cashier, 'Put this on our bill, please.' Then she turned, smiled at Ginger and said to her sister, 'Shall we go, dear?' and without another word they left the building and climbed into a cab which had miraculously appeared outside on Sansome Street just as they emerged.

3

As she drove south down the Peninsula, Ginger rehearsed her list of questions for Harlan Taylor, the president of Taylor Technology. After lunch with the Dillon twins, she had phoned him for an appointment, wanting reassurance his company would increase its earnings two-fold by the end of the second quarter.

She had had no doubts about the company the last time she made that trip. Her sudden doubts were the direct result of Neil Cameron's accepting her rash promise to return his brokerage commission personally if the stock didn't perform well.

There was no point in berating herself once more about that bit of insanity. She had said it, he had taken her challenge and there was nothing to do now but accept her fate with whatever good grace she could muster. In fact, there was really no point in going back to the firm to look it over again. After all, she couldn't raise their earnings herself merely by visiting the place. She knew it was a reaction on her part, a desperate ploy to assure herself she hadn't been completely absurd.

She parked her car in the lot and entered the cool, air conditioned office building. The room seemed dark after the bright sunlight outdoors, and she stood at the reception desk a moment, letting her eyes adjust.

'Please be seated,' the girl said after she gave her name. 'He'll be with you in a moment.'

She turned toward the chairs in the waiting area, and a man rose in front of her, startling her. Cameron.

'You!' she stammered. 'What are you doing here?'

'The same as you, apparently.' He took her hand in his. 'And how are you this afternoon?'

Surprised into inability to say another

word, Ginger allowed him to lead her to a chair, wondering if her wildly beating heart could be heard as well as felt.

Releasing her hand, he sat beside her and spoke in a soft, confidential tone. 'I didn't expect to see you. Didn't you tell me in your office this morning that you had visited Harlan Taylor only two weeks ago?'

'Yes,' Ginger said, her face feeling uncomfortably warm under his searching gaze. 'I did visit him recently.'

'Then why are you back again? Is it possible you weren't as confident of your findings as you led me to believe?' His words were serious, but his eyes sparkled with merriment.

Her voice as low as his, she said, 'No, it's not. I'm sure the company's earnings will double, just as I told you.'

'Then why — ?'

'Thank you for your interest, Mr. Cameron,' she said, 'but my reasons for being here are — are — confidential.' Well, they were. She'd been sworn to secrecy by his very own aunts.

'Please,' he said, taking her hand in his again. 'I thought we were going to be Ginger and Mac.'

'You may call me whatever you like, but you're my client and I don't think I should be so informal.' She pulled her hand free, as much to establish the distance between them as to hide the fact that it was hot and trembling from his touch.

Then she remembered her surprise at finding him there. 'Speaking of reasons, why are you here? Did you follow me?'

'Not at all. Believe me, I'm as surprised as you that we both turned up here this afternoon.'

'You had no interest in the company this morning.'

'I pride myself on being open-minded. Since you sounded so sure of your facts, I thought I might have been hasty in believing someone else's account. I decided to see for myself.'

'In that case, perhaps I should leave.' She started to rise, wondering why her emotions seemed so contrary. She wanted to stay, yet he seemed to confuse her with every word.

He restrained her with a firm grasp on her arm. 'Why do that? Let me be the one to leave.'

'No, that isn't necessary. After all, I've visited the company before and you haven't. I really think you should talk to Taylor. I think he'll convince you just as he did me.'

'I didn't mean to offend you. I'm sorry. I really didn't think you would be upset by my coming. Look here — '

But whatever he was about to say was cut short by the approach of Harlan Taylor, a balding man in his late thirties, with horn-rimmed glasses, a thin face and tall, angular body.

'Hello, Mrs. Maddox,' he said jovially. Then, turning to Cameron, he said, 'Mac, old man, it's good to see you again — '

Ginger felt a knot in her stomach. Just what was going on? Cameron and Taylor were obviously friends; yet he'd been unwilling at first even to consider their stock.

'You two know each other?' Taylor asked.

Since there was no good reason to leave then, Ginger answered. 'Mr. Cameron and I met in my office this morning. He allowed me to persuade him to buy stock in your company, and now, quite by chance, we both turned up here this afternoon.'

'That's wonderful,' Taylor said smoothly, apparently not concerned about who had persuaded whom. 'I can take you both around on a tour of the plant. You've never seen it, Mac, but I hope you'll be impressed.'

As they surveyed the plant, Ginger felt excluded from most of the conversation. Through room after room of workers assembling parts, through laboratories where white-coated men and women peered into microscopes, through rooms of computers and large well-lighted offices, Taylor explained procedures and answered questions by

Ginger's unexpected companion.

She didn't really mind their ignoring her. She had, after all, had this tour before, so part of her brain didn't need to think about it. Instead, she tried to understand why Cameron had been so reluctant at first to consider Taylor stock. What little game was he playing? She thought, too, of his two aunts and the games they were playing, the secrecy. Were all the people in his family so mysterious about their business and their lives?

Walking beside the tall, arrestingly handsome man, watching him when he wasn't aware of it, hearing him speak, ask intelligent questions, she couldn't help being impressed. She was aware too of another feeling, as if there was more than coincidence involved in their turning up there at the same time. Her heart began to beat more strongly and her skin tingled.

Almost an hour later, they were back in the receptionist's lobby saying goodbye, and Taylor returned to his office.

'May I drop you somewhere?' Cameron asked her.

'No, I have my own car.'

He held the building door open for her, and she started across the parking lot. To her surprise, he followed.

'Then you can drop me,' he said.

'I beg your pardon?' She stopped and they almost collided.

'I don't have a car yet,' he said. 'I came down on the Southern Pacific and then took a cab to the plant.'

After a pause, while she absorbed this information, she said, 'Of course you're welcome to a ride back.' Resuming her walk to her blue Ford Escort, she told herself she was only being polite; yet somehow she was glad to extend her time with him. She couldn't deny the sudden lift in her spirits. 'Where are you staying in the city?'

'At the Fairmont, for the moment. I'm looking for a house or apartment to rent. Eventually, I'd like to buy some property.'

Ginger unlocked the car door and he

held it open for her. As she settled into the driver's seat, she was aware of his gaze scanning her legs. Then he went around and got in beside her. She felt all thumbs as she inserted the key in the ignition and started it, then maneuvered the car out of the parking lot.

'I'm very impressed with Taylor Technology,' he said when they were smoothly integrated into the traffic of the freeway.

'Are you really?'

'I have the feeling you doubt me,' he answered lightly. 'Where have I gone wrong?'

'For openers, how about that little charade in my office this morning? Pretending you didn't know anything nice about Taylor?' Ginger waited for his reply, her gaze straight ahead.

After a pause he said, 'I guess that was rather foolish of me. You're far too perceptive a person to be taken in. At any rate, you would have found out sooner or later.'

'Well?'

'Let's keep it for later, shall we?'

'What is it you're hiding?' She felt annoyed with his secrecy. 'If it's anything I ought to know about, anything illegal or unethical — '

'No, no,' he assured her. 'Nothing like that. You'll have to trust me that I wouldn't do anything to hurt you.'

His choice of words made Ginger even more suspicious. What did he mean by not 'hurting' her? Somehow that made it sound more ominous, as if there were more at stake than investment money.

She kept her voice even. 'I suppose I can't force you to tell me what it is. The broker-client relationship ought to be one of mutual trust and confidence. As you know, millions of dollars' worth of stock change hands every day with only a telephone call to seal the bargain.'

'I'm aware of that. Again, all I can say is that I haven't told you any lies — I never said I *didn't* know Harlan Taylor — and you have nothing to fear.'

Frustrated, Ginger realized her foot

trod too heavily on the accelerator and she lifted it. Deliberately relaxing, and telling herself she might as well not worry about it, since she could do nothing anyway, she changed the subject.

'How long have you been in San Francisco?'

'A little over a week.'

'How do you like it, so far?'

'It's all that I expected, and more. I've been to southern California before, but never to 'Frisco. I must say it is every bit as charming as I'd been led to believe.'

Ginger corrected him. 'Excuse me. We never say 'Frisco.' It stamps you as an outsider immediately.'

'I'll remember that. A bit touchy, don't you think?'

'It has to do with the early days of the city. During the time of the gold rush, it was rather a bawdy place and the sailors called it 'Frisco'; so the bankers, railroad men and so forth, made it a point not to use that expression.

Residents have never used it from that day to this.'

'How interesting. Are you a treasure trove of San Francisco history?'

Ginger couldn't help smiling at that. 'Not really. I do know a little. Frankly, I find it fascinating.'

'I'll look forward to hearing more one day.'

Again Ginger flashed a look at her passenger and wondered what he meant, and then told herself she was overreacting. But his next words removed her doubt.

'Will you have dinner with me tonight?'

'No, I'm sorry. The New York Stock Exchange opens three hours ahead of us so I get up extremely early.'

'It's not even six. And you have to eat sometime. I don't mind dining early if that's better for you.'

Ginger considered it. On one hand she enjoyed his company and something inside her was reluctant to end the moment. Yet, she was nervous. She had been out with a man only once since Colin's death and that was with the brother of an old school chum who happened to be in town. She had a sensation, this time, of being somehow disloyal to Colin's memory to have anything resembling a date.

Still silent, Ginger saw her exit approaching and pulled off the freeway onto the city streets. Traffic was heavy and, as she maneuvered her car toward Nob Hill, they literally crept along.

'You didn't answer my question,' he reminded her. 'What are you afraid of?'

Afraid? She bristled at the thought. It certainly wasn't that. She was always in control of herself and her emotions. Having dinner with a man was not necessarily an invitation to anything else.

'Very well,' she said at last. 'The Crown Room here has a nice view, although no doubt you've seen it already.'

'As a matter of fact, I have, but it was

dark at the time. I'm sure the view is different during the day.'

'I'll park the car.'

'Let the doorman do it for you,' Cameron said, and with that, he stepped from the car which Ginger had stopped in the curving entrance, said a few words to the uniformed man, and then helped her out. Still silent, they crossed the elegant lobby and went up in the elevator to the Crown Room, where they were given a window table. The air was clear and they looked out on a vast view of the city, the waters of the bay and the hills beyond.

After they ordered, he said, 'Tell me about yourself.'

'There's not much to tell,' she answered. 'I graduated from Stanford, as Mr. Blake told you, I married right out of college and now I work in the brokerage office.'

'Blake indicated your husband died rather tragically.'

'I'd really rather not talk about that.' He had brought back painful memories of Colin's death that she preferred to forget.

'What about you? You said you were from the East.' She looked into his warm brown eyes.

'Boston,' he answered. 'I was born and raised there, then attended a very small private college in the Midwest.'

'That explains why you have no Eastern accent.'

'I pick up accents wherever I am; but I think the Midwestern accent is almost universal in this country. However, if I spent ten days in Birmingham, Alabama, I dare say I would go about saying 'you-all' like a native.'

Ginger laughed, and felt a relaxation creep into her body. Or was it the pleasant surroundings that soothed her?

As if intuition told him she felt more comfortable, he pressed her again for details about her life. 'Did you major in business in college; is that how one prepares for a career as a stock broker?'

'Actually, I never expected to be a

representative. I majored in library science until I met Colin and then switched over. He was a great help to me.'

'I suspect that, as a member of Mensa, you didn't find that a big problem.' A disarming smile made crinkly lines around his eyes.

'You've heard of Mensa, then? Most people haven't. Not that it matters.' She shrugged.

'An organization for people with I.Q.s in the top two per cent of the population, about 133, I believe.'

'You're very well informed.' She fingered the napkin in her lap while she studied his face, looking for a reason he might have remembered such a thing. 'Or are you a member, too?'

'No.' His full-throated laugh rang through the elegant cocktail lounge. 'I haven't time to join organizations.'

'One doesn't join,' Ginger corrected, 'that is, not exactly. I had to take a test — I did it at Stanford, as a matter of fact — and they told me I passed. There are local chapters which meet regularly, I believe, and do things together, but I've never attended any of the meetings.'

'What's the purpose then?' His face had turned more serious now, as if he really wanted to know.

'I did participate in one thing: a questionnaire in which we were asked our opinions on some important issues.'

'That sounds interesting.' He leaned across the table toward her as if to take her hand, but just then the waiter brought their dinner. Ginger was glad for the interruption; she felt uncomfortable talking about herself and she was learning nothing about him. He was the mysterious one. 'What did you do after college?'

'I traveled around for a while. I like to think I hold the record for having stayed in the most youth hostels in Europe. Then I married too.' He paused and Ginger feared he would say no more, so she prompted him.

'And — '

'Darlene was an actress, excuse me, is an actress — '

'She must be both beautiful and intelligent,' Ginger said. 'Acting requires a lot of study.'

'Actresses are not necessarily beautiful,' he said, looking directly into her eyes for a long time. 'In this case, however, it was true.' After another pause, he continued without further urging. 'We moved to New York to help her career, and I became involved in the investment community that hovers around Wall Street. Then the marriage broke up.'

'Just like that?' Ginger's voice had dropped to a whisper.

'Just about like that. She found her career more attractive than marriage.' As if the subject were closed, he tackled his steak with vigor and she did the same, letting the background music replace their conversation.

Ginger broke the silence. 'She must be famous by now. Would I have heard of her? Darlene what?'

'She's not Darlene anymore. She changed her name to Darryl Winthrop and, last I heard, she was doing rather well.' He shifted in his chair, as if uncomfortable.

'I didn't mean to pry,' Ginger said, catching his mood. 'As a matter of fact, I think I've heard of her. Didn't she have a part in that Chicago gangster play last year?'

'Yes, I believe she did. You have a remarkable memory if you can recall the names of the bit players.'

'Oh, it was more than a bit part. But you're right, I do tend to remember things like that. Colin always accused me of having a head stuffed with trivia.' This time the mention of his name didn't seem to hurt. Jim Blake had always told her not to block out his memory completely, that talking about him would eventually ease the pain.

'It's a pretty head,' Cameron said, once more leaning toward her. 'And the stuffing doesn't show at all.'

Again they laughed.

'What kinds of investing did you do while you were in New York?' she pressed.

'Oh, we're not going to talk business, are we?' He turned his head to the view of San Francisco through the wide windows. The sky was darkening to shades of blue and purple. 'I want to know more about your city. What do you do on your days off?'

'Clean my apartment,' she joked. 'In the beginning, that is, when Colin and I first moved here — ' She paused, realizing she had again spoken Colin's name without anguish. ' — we did all the tourist things, rode the cable cars, took cruises to Sausalito and Alcatraz, hiked Mt. Tamalpais. On summer Sunday afternoons, we attended the free concerts in Stern Grove or Golden Gate Park.'

'That sounds wonderful. Perhaps you and I will do those things together,' he said. Again his eyes searched hers.

Ginger returned suddenly to reality. No, they would not do those things together. It was one thing to be able to have dinner with a man without guilt, even talk about Colin without pain, but she had no intention of getting involved with anyone yet, certainly not a complete stranger, and a mysterious one at that.

'It's getting late,' she said, ignoring the coffee that the waiter set in front of them. 'I really should go.'

'If you must.' He asked for the bill, signed it, and helped Ginger from her chair. They walked to the lobby, he tipped the doorman and again helped her into the car, then went around and got in beside her.

Surprised, she stared at him.

'A gentleman always sees a lady home. I'll take a cab back. Besides, I want to see where you live. Or, did you have other plans?' He looked at her innocently.

'Not unless you consider washing my hair a plan.' She slipped the car into traffic and headed for her apartment, silent, her thoughts going in circles.

Finally she pulled into her driveway, the garage door opener raised the single expanse of solid wood, and she pulled inside. They got out of the car and returned to the sidewalk.

The sun behind the buildings created deep shadows, and Ginger could barely see Cameron's face.

'It's been an interesting day,' he said. 'You'll forgive the cliche if I say I feel as if I've known you much longer than ten hours.'

The balmy breeze of evening ruffled Ginger's hair. She too, felt as if she had known him more than ten hours. Somehow she felt she should apologize for her abrupt departure from the Crown Room, for overreacting to his suggestion they might do things together. After all, they were going to be business associates. Perhaps he meant nothing by his remarks. He could merely want to be a friend. Did she want him for a friend? Or more?

He stepped closer, squashing the friendship idea. She knew at once what would happen and felt powerless to prevent it, unable to decide if she even wanted to. His hands held her gently by the shoulders, his head lowered to hers, and he kissed her on her slightly parted lips. At once a searing fire went through her body, as if his touch had ignited a spark that had lain dormant too long. A huge dose of guilt swept over her. Yet, at the same time, she enjoyed the warm smoothness of his lips on hers.

A car drove down the street, and they broke apart. Eyes open once more, Ginger's defenses came into place again.

'Mr. Cameron — '

'Please,' he began. 'You were going to call me 'Mac'.'

She shook her head. 'Somehow you don't seem like a 'Mac'. Since you're so insistent that we be on a first-name basis I'll call you Neil. But you mustn't — '

It was his turn to look surprised and his dark brows arched. 'How did you know I prefer that name?'

She was about to say, 'Your aunts use it,' but then remembered the ladies' admonition. She returned, instead, to the incident of his kiss.

'You're trying to change the subject,' she said. 'You really — I mean, we can't have a business relationship if you — '

'I know,' he said. 'It wasn't fair of me. But I've been wanting to do that ever since I met you this morning.'

Ginger's eyes widened. Ever since this morning? Was it possible he meant that?

'Don't worry,' he added. 'I won't let it happen again. I don't want to jeopardize our — friendship. I shall be a perfect gentleman, and won't ask to come inside, even if you are the most beautiful woman I've seen in San Francisco.'

Still silent, Ginger backed away from him, but he caught one hand for an instant and pressed it.

'Good night,' he said in a husky voice.

'Good night,' Ginger turned and

started up the steps, not waiting to see if he caught a cab at the corner. She hoped he couldn't tell that her legs, feeling as weak as cooked spaghetti, wobbled as she went.

4

Saturday was no longer Ginger's favorite day. When she was a child, it had been because she had no school or homework. She would be up early, running across the back yard, out the gate and then down the road to play with friends. Her mop of bright hair bobbing, she would lead them on exploring trips, or encourage them to put on a show of some sort. Sometimes it would be a circus, and they'd bring their dogs and cats dressed up in old clothes, and put paper streamers on their doll carriages or tricycles for a parade.

After she met Colin at college, and especially after they married, Saturday was a most cherished day. They spent almost every moment together, sometimes with Jim Blake sailing on the bay. But that was over; Colin was gone.

Suddenly Neil Cameron came to her mind. What occupied him on Saturdays as a child? What was he doing today? His kissing her brought a blush to her cheeks again. The memory of how she had enjoyed that kiss, which she had been trying so hard to forget since then, insisted on coming forward. But she felt guilty too. Neil was a client and if you were smart, you simply did not get involved with clients. Furthermore, how could she even think of responding to another man's kiss when she and Colin had been so happily married? Even to imagine a romance with someone else made her feel like a traitor.

She dismissed Neil Cameron and thought of Jim Blake. This was the day of his housewarming party. He had just moved into a new condominium on Cathedral Hill and had invited most of the representatives from the stock brokerage, as well as other friends. Ginger was looking forward to it, even though she hoped they wouldn't talk shop all evening.

With that, she slipped out of bed, pulled on jeans and a tee-shirt, and set about doing her Saturday chores, shopping for groceries for the coming week, picking up her dry cleaning and straightening her apartment. Then she dressed for the party.

Turning this way and that before the full-length mirror in her bedroom, she admired her new dress. It was floor length, with a soft, draped skirt that hung gracefully about her legs, and its top was shirred into a Grecian style, with a deep cowled neckline. The fabric narrowed over the shoulders, leaving most of her back and all of her arms bare. Next, she put on high-heeled matching silk sandals and her full-length velvet evening coat. Its deep blue color looked almost black in the folds, while the creases seemed light blue, matching the dress.

Jim's white Cadillac picked her up in front of her apartment ten minutes later. She had protested when he first suggested it, but it was pleasant not to have to worry about finding a cab, or a parking place if she drove herself. Jim stepped out, hugged her, and then went around to the passenger side and helped her into the car. 'My dear Ginger, you look stunning tonight.'

'Thanks, Jim, you get an A-plus for compliments.'

The car pulled smoothly away from the curb before Jim spoke again. 'Just because I'm picking you up, don't think I intend to take you home again. There are some eligible men coming tonight who ought to receive that honor.'

'Thanks, but no thanks. I'll take a cab.'

'As a matter of fact, I had another reason for wanting these few minutes alone with you. It's been a secret up to now, but tonight you're going to meet my girlfriend.'

'Your girlfriend?' Ginger repeated. 'You're right; that is a secret. I didn't know you were seeing anyone.'

'Well,' Jim said, 'I'm not quite sure

how serious this is going to be. I guess I'm saying I'd like your opinion.'

'I'm certainly flattered,' Ginger said, 'but — '

'You know the old saying, 'once bit, twice shy.' I don't want to make another mistake if I can help it.'

'I can understand that, but friends can often hold a completely different impression of someone, one that's not exactly accurate. My opinion might be worthless.'

'We've been friends so long, I respect your judgment.'

'I'd be happy to meet her, but you really shouldn't expect anything more. I didn't pass judgment on your first wife and I see no reason why I should start doing that now.'

The car slowed as they climbed a steep hill, and then they pulled into the underground garage of a tall white building. Jim parked the car and they took the elevator to his floor.

'Speaking of girlfriends,' Jim said, as the elevator rose, 'I wish you'd find someone, so you wouldn't be attending parties alone. I loved Colin like a brother, but it's been a year — '

'I know, but I'm not in any hurry. In fact, I may never marry again. Unlike you, I have no unpleasant memories of a failed marriage. Mine was wonderful. I can't imagine anyone else who could ever make me so happy again.'

Jim was silent for a moment. 'I hope you're not idolizing Colin. He was a fine person, and I'm glad you were happy with him, but he wasn't perfect. No one is. You can be happy again — you ought to be — but if you start canonizing Colin, you'll never find anyone who will live up to your mental image of him.'

Neil Cameron's face flashed before Ginger's eyes. She thrust away the image at once. Even if she were to consider finding someone to take Colin's place, Neil would not be in the running. He was too much of a puzzle, one she didn't care to unravel.

'Thanks for your concern,' Ginger

said, 'but please don't worry. I can take care of myself.'

'Hmmm. Maybe that's what I'm afraid of.'

The elevator door opened and they stepped into the corridor and walked down its carpeted length. Jim opened a door. His living room was partly filled with guests already, but Ginger could see that the apartment was modern, spacious and beautiful. Mirrors covered one complete wall to the left, against which stood a polished black credenza. In front, a wall of glass revealed the twinkling lights of the city below. To the right were white sofas, forest green chairs, glass-topped tables trimmed with shiny chrome, and huge potted plants, whose leaves matched the velvet of the chairs as if they'd been dyed for the occasion. Jim had a wonderful personality *and* exquisite taste.

Taking her coat with him, he disappeared down a hallway, calling over his shoulder, 'You know everyone, don't you?'

Ginger greeted two representatives from the office and their wives, chatted with them for a few moments and then leaned over to sample the canapes on the coffee table in front of one of the white sofas.

'There are some hot ones in the dining room.' The voice belonged to Neil Cameron who stood behind her.

He wore a black tuxedo, black tie, and pleated white shirt, and seemed even taller than she remembered. 'Hello,' she said, grateful her hands were occupied — one with a small plate and the other with a cheese-topped tidbit — so that she didn't have to shake hands with him. Even without his touch, she was only too easily reminded that the last time she'd seen him he had ended their meeting with a kiss, and the mere thought of it was making her face feel warm and her scalp tight.

'You are even more beautiful than the last time I saw you, if that's possible,' he said.

'Thank you. I see you're making

friends in San Francisco.'

'Yes, Jim Blake was kind enough to invite me tonight. We had a nice chat yesterday and seem to have a lot in common.'

Yesterday? Neil had come into the office Friday? He must have gone straight to Jim's office. Why?

'You weren't complaining about me again, were you?' she teased, remembering his first reaction when they met.

'By no means. In fact, we didn't mention you at all.'

Ginger was relieved. She had no wish for Jim to know they had been to Taylor Technology together, had dinner and ended their meeting with a kiss.

'I asked his advice about finding a place to live,' Neil continued, 'and he suggested I come tonight so that I could see this building. He says there are still a few units available.'

'It's very attractive,' Ginger said, looking around the spacious room.

'It is indeed. I might like it as a San Francisco address.'

66

'Just as a San Francisco address? Does that mean you aren't going to make this your permanent home after all?'

'The bay area, yes. I meant I might like to have a home in the suburbs too. They tell me Marin County is lovely. Besides, I'm enchanted with your Golden Gate Bridge, and the thought of being able to drive across it every day intrigues me.'

'It's just a bridge,' she said. 'We actually have several.'

'Just a bridge? You underestimate it. Some of the greatest bridge builders in the world have commented on it. In fact, the Bay Bridge has been described as 'merely a span'.'

'You know a lot about the bay area suddenly. Have you been boning up lately?'

He smiled and Ginger again felt her heart begin to beat strongly. Why did his smile always do that to her?

'My aunts,' he said. 'They've lived here most of their lives. Like you,

67

they're veritable storehouses of information about San Francisco. I visited them most of the day.'

So that was where he'd been while Ginger was wondering how he spent his Saturday. She liked the vision she conjured of him with the two eccentric ladies, sitting at their feet while they told him stories of the old city.

'It reminded me,' he continued, 'of the little boy who wrote a review of the book about penguins. He said, 'It told me more about penguins than I wanted to know.''

Ginger laughed. 'So do you feel that you know more about San Francisco than you really cared to know?'

'Somewhat, all in one session. I'd prefer to have it spread out a little. In fact, I was rather hoping to learn more of it from you. I enjoyed our — conversation.'

Recalling his kiss was dangerous to Ginger's peace of mind and she changed the subject. 'Didn't you say something about hot *hors d'oeuvres* in the dining room?'

'I did. This way.' He went before her, making a path through the crowd, which by now had become considerably larger. Her progress was impeded, however, by numbers of people, as well as stopping to say hello to friends. By the time she reached the dining room, where several hot dishes were displayed on a smoky glass-topped table, Neil had apparently filled his own plate and disappeared. Refusing to be disappointed, Ginger sampled some of the food, accepted a glass of wine and then found Jim Blake.

'Where's your girlfriend?' she asked. 'I don't intend to pass judgment, but I do want to meet her.'

Jim pointed with his glass, and Ginger saw a willowy blonde dressed in green satin. Like the ficus trees and huge schefflera plants, she matched the decor.

'How long have you known her?' Ginger asked.

'Seven months. She's wonderful:

bright, beautiful, divorced, but no children. I'd have asked her to marry me weeks ago, but frankly, I'm scared.'

'Scared of what?'

'Angie was beautiful and bright too, and that was a disaster. Does anyone ever know beforehand if it's right?'

'Bright and beautiful are obviously not enough. Do you like the same things?'

'Oh sure. We both play golf, love sailing, the ballet.'

'Sounds as if you're compatible,' Ginger encouraged.

'I hope so.' He ran his hand across his chin.

'Are you going to ask her soon?'

'I'm still thinking. I'm certainly nervous about it. I handle million-dollar deals with less concern than this.'

Ginger laughed gently. 'That's natural, deals involve only money. I'll give you some of the advice you gave me driving over: don't wait for perfection.'

'That's just the trouble, she's too perfect. I think that's what worries me.

I keep asking myself, 'Why hasn't someone else snatched her up by now?''

'You said she was recently divorced.'

'No, not recently, about five years ago.'

'Well, perhaps, like you, she's been waiting for the right person to come along.'

'But there are certainly men who are better looking than I am: thinner — ' He paused and touched his glass to his slightly protruding middle, then continued, ' — more money — '

'You're a great guy, Jim. Just be glad that she thinks so too. By the way, what's her name?'

'Cynthia.'

'That's a pretty name and suits her.' Ginger patted his arm. She didn't want to spend the evening reassuring him that he wasn't about to make another mistake. She had no way of knowing, even if she knew Cynthia. Only time could prove if it was the right step or not.

How would she feel if someone asked her to marry him? Would she go through the same agony that Jim was apparently suffering? A sudden vision of Neil Cameron on bended knee made her laugh inwardly. *That* would never happen.

'Come on,' she told Jim, 'it's time I met her.'

He steered her forward and introduced them. After a short conversation, more guests joined them. Suddenly a strange feeling came over Ginger. It was as if she had been there before, seen those people before, said the same things before. She knew in advance, like a playwright, what everyone was going to say and do. The subject changed and she heard every word that was spoken and even added comments herself, all the while feeling that all of this had happened some other time, in some other life. She glanced up and locked eyes with Neil. She knew he was going to come to her and say, 'Let's go, shall we?' and they would leave. It was what the French called *deja vu,* but knowing that didn't erase the eerie feeling.

Then, a couple who had been standing next to her suddenly turned away from Ginger and began to talk to Jim. Neil stood in front of her. 'Let's go, shall we?'

5

Ginger let Neil lead her down the hall where the open door of a yellow bedroom revealed a bed laden with guests' coats. Hers was on top of the pile, and he held it for her while her arms found the sleeves. Somewhere inside a voice whispered that she shouldn't do it, but at the same time she felt powerless to change the scenario. Back in the living room, heading for the door, Ginger wondered how she would ever say goodnight to Jim without seeming a complete fool, but Neil solved that problem too. 'We're going for a walk,' he told her boss, and propelled her out of the apartment before either of them could say more.

The spell that had somehow been cast over her wasn't broken until they reached the street and the fresh cold air fanned her face. Then everything became normal again, the future unknown.

They walked down the slanted sidewalk that descended the hill, over curbs and across streets, his hand clasping hers securely. The city was indescribably beautiful, the air crystal clear and the sky dark with a myriad of twinkling stars. Even the tall buildings seemed warm and friendly.

'Your city seems to have limitless charms,' Neil said. 'I can't decide if I prefer it in daytime or the evening.'

'I feel that way sometimes myself.'

'But you've always known it. I should think you'd be jaded by now. Or is San Francisco a city that never bores its inhabitants?'

'First of all, I'm not really a native. I was born in Pacific Grove and didn't come to the bay area until I went to Stanford. And, secondly, I think you're right. I do believe San Francisco is the only city where the natives take nothing for granted, and enjoy it every bit as much as the tourists.'

'That's a wonderful thing to say about a city.'

'Please,' she laughed, 'you'll have me sounding like the Chamber of Commerce.'

He pulled her hand back so that her body turned slightly in his direction and he could look at her. 'I want to get to know your city better. And I especially want to know you better.' He swung her arm back again. 'That's why I kidnapped you from the party.' His voice was very low.

'You make it sound rather ominous,' Ginger said.

'I might as well be honest, I have every intention — '

Before he could finish the sentence, Ginger interrupted. Warnings flashed in her head. Had she allowed Neil to rescue her from the party only to have him behave the way he had the other day? 'I only want to be friends, nothing more.'

'I don't see how that's going to be

possible. You must know by now that I'm tremendously attracted to you.'

'You made that clear Wednesday evening,' Ginger said, 'but we also agreed it wasn't wise to mix business with pleasure.'

'Then you admit our getting to know one another better could be pleasure.' He grinned mischievously.

Ginger felt warm, her face tingled. 'I didn't say that. I only meant we must keep our personal lives separate.'

'I feel exactly the same way. I promise not to kiss you in your office.'

She had to smile, in spite of the danger signals that swarmed, like bees, in her stomach. 'You're twisting my meaning. I can't, I won't, become involved with anyone.'

'You don't intend to live out your life as a lonely spinster, do you?'

'Whether I do or not is really none of your business, you know. Please — ' She pulled her hand from his and thrust it into the pocket of her wrap. ' — let's not talk about it.'

Unaware they had been walking in that direction, Ginger found herself in front of her own door. She looked at Neil. 'You certainly learned your way around the city in a hurry.'

'Oh, didn't I tell you? I'm part homing pigeon.'

'But this time it's *my* home.'

'So much the better. You wanted to get here eventually, didn't you?' He took the key from her hands, unlocked the door, and after they climbed the stairs, unlocked her apartment door.

'May I come in?'

'Of course. I didn't mean to sound hostile. We can be friends.'

'Spare me,' he said, raising a hand. 'Let's not start that again. We seem to be talking in circles.' He helped her out of her coat and draped it over a chair while she turned on lamps.

'I should rent a car, I suppose, while I'm shopping for one. I'm afraid it was cruel of me to make you walk all this way.'

'I didn't mind, although I think I'd

like to take my shoes off.' She smiled, glad he had changed the subject.

She stepped out of the sandals and then he led her to the sofa in front of the fireplace. 'Do you mind if I light this?' Without waiting for a reply, he turned on the gas jet and lit the logs.

'It's only a fake one.' She felt foolish stating the obvious, but in spite of his comradely demeanor, she was beginning to feel threatened again. It had been foolish to invite him in. How could he trust her words that she wanted no involvement if she let him share, even this small amount, in her private world? Somehow she must keep everything impersonal. 'Would you like something? Coffee?' She started to rise.

'Nothing,' he answered, and catching her hand again, pressed her back into the seat once more. Instead of sitting next to her, however, he sat on the floor at her feet, his back against her knees, his head near her lap. 'Let's just enjoy the fire.'

The silence was comfortable and the

feel of his broad back against her legs was somehow not imprisoning, but reassuring and even, yes, friendly. She had an almost irresistible urge to run her fingers through the thick mahogany hair so close to her touch. Would it feel coarse or smooth?

'This is so peaceful,' he said, 'I could stay here forever.' Then he turned around and looked at her.

She was amazed to see a sad look in his eyes. 'What's the matter?' she asked. She felt a rising tide of emotion coming over her again.

He didn't answer and the sadness in his eyes vanished at once. Graceful as a cat, he unfolded his long frame from his position on the floor and sat beside her. One arm reached along the sofa back and stopped, inches from her shoulders.

'I can't remember when I've felt so comfortable.'

She looked away. She must pull herself together. This was becoming far too dangerous. She could not become involved with this man.

'You really must leave now,' she said. The words were automatic and she knew, even as she spoke, that neither would act on them. The knot in her stomach dissolved the instant his arms went around her. Then his mouth descended on hers. The kiss was light, firm, but not passionate.

When he broke the kiss, she said, 'I'm sorry.' But her voice sounded strange, like someone else's voice. 'I shouldn't have let you kiss me. You'd better leave.'

'In a moment.' He leaned toward her again. His arm dropped to her shoulder and its heat started fires in the pit of her stomach. Pressing gently, he brought her to him, and his other hand touched her cheek, then stole behind her ear, his fingers mingling with the strands of her hair.

His face came closer, firelight dancing on his skin, changing his profile from second to second, unreal, mysterious.

'Please go,' she said again, her voice

an ineffective cry from common sense, but his lips descended on hers, cutting short her words. The knot in her stomach dissolved the instant his mouth made contact. Of their own accord, her arms went around his waist, holding him close.

His right hand slid from her neck and pressed the small of her back, bringing her even closer. Then it stole to her hips, at the same time he murmured between kisses, 'Ginger, my darling.'

Reality crept in with his words, tiny at first, then growing. 'Don't,' she whispered, 'we must stop. This is — '

'In a moment.' Not releasing her, his words were almost inaudible.

Their thoughts seemed to be running tandem, for hers admitted, in her deepest self, that she needed more of his touch. 'You must leave now.'

'Your body speaks more eloquently for you,' he said, one finger tracing the outline of her lips.

She pulled herself from his embrace with difficulty. As if in a dream that she knew, however unwillingly, she must wake from, she rose from the sofa and walked softly across the room to the window and sat on the velvet padded window seat. She traced a finger over the mullioned panes, barely aware that the fog had come in and blotted out the view, obscuring the houses across the street and even the leaves of the tall tree that stood in its solitary rectangle of earth below her window.

He came up behind her silently and stood close, close enough to touch, yet not touching her. He seemed to be waiting.

The words she wanted to say — a repetition of why they could not become emotionally entangled when they were to be business associates — lay behind her lips but refused to emerge. Instead, once more, she seemed helpless before the coming moment.

His hands began to caress her arms and shoulders. He kissed the back of her neck, his breath warm on her skin.

She tilted her head back, felt her hair brush against his shirt front. Gently, he turned her toward him. He kissed her passionately this time and she didn't resist.

He held her body tightly to his and she put her arms around him and pressed him close, The world disappeared, leaving only this fantasy. Did he feel the same thing? Was this sense of being suspended in time and space the same for him?

The sweet pressure of his lips released a pent-up emotion. Fevered kisses warmed her mouth. They pressed, coaxing, savoring her, like a starving creature. Seconds turned into minutes, breaths mingled, tongues colliding in hunger for more of each other. When finally his lips left hers, they traveled to her cheeks, her chin, her throat, his tongue probing the pulse at the base of her neck.

She felt the filmy straps of her dress move across her shoulders and fall onto her arms, while his hands caressed the creamy skin of her neck and shoulders.

Yes, yes, a voice within her said. Helpless before her unexpected response, mesmerized by the haunting force of the evening and the spell he had cast, she couldn't stop. This had never happened to her before and yet she felt it was a love scene repeated out of a memory. She would have it, the voice promised.

She pressed him closer, fingers woven in his thick hair. His lips traced the path his hands had taken, sending stabs of desire into every corner of her being.

Suddenly her mind wrested control away from the voice and began its protest. 'Please,' she gasped, her breath ragged.

Neil's voice was hoarse as if he, too, were experiencing sudden emotions. 'I won't do anything you don't want me to,' he whispered, 'but you know you want this as much as I do.'

'Stop, please stop.' The words were barely audible, yet she knew that another moment of his touch on her trembling body might sweep her over the edge. From what depths of desire had this wanton response appeared? She had met him only *days* ago.

His voice became husky. 'I've been obsessed by you since the moment I first saw you. When you looked so defensive and yet so adorable.' He nuzzled her neck.

'And then offering to repay my commissions — ' His voice took on a lighter, humorous tone, with a deep chuckle. 'You don't have to do that, you know.'

At once the dream-like sensations of the evening came to a halt, like a bubble bursting, and she was back in control. What did he say about the commissions she promised to repay? What did he mean, 'you don't have to do that'? Like a bolt of lightning, it suddenly became clear. He was suggesting that if she let him make love to her, he would forget her promise. He was bargaining with her, bribing her.

She pushed him away, anger rising in her like bile. How could he even think such a thing, assume she would sell her body in exchange for the broker's commission?

She felt she would explode and her voice rose shrilly. 'How dare you?'

Neil's expression changed into one of disbelief, then shock and anger, mirroring her own feelings. 'What do you mean? How dare I what? What are you talking about?'

'I admit you had me at the brink of — ' She couldn't say it, even to herself.

He shook his head. 'Are you objecting to my lovemaking?' His eyes glared through her like piercing dark swords.

'I did,' Ginger insisted, trying to vindicate herself. 'I asked you to leave. I moved away from you.'

'Only to melt against me the moment I touched you.' The lines of his face were etched with stress.

'You're twisting things,' she protested, her fury increasing. 'That's despicable enough, but to actually assume that I would let you make love to me to keep from acknowledging a financial obligation — '

'What financial obligation?' Neil countered, looking straight into her eyes, towering over her.

'Oh, isn't that what this was all about?'

'You mean my kissing you? Do I need a reason for wanting to make love to you? Don't you think I'm human, with normal men's desires?'

'I don't mean that,' she panted, flustered, struggling to keep to the point, 'you said I didn't have to repay your commissions as I promised.'

He was silent for a moment, a frown creasing his forehead, as if only then beginning to understand what had upset her. 'You think — you actually think — I would attempt to bribe you into a love affair?'

Her indignation began to wither. Something about the way he said it made it sound as if she doubted he had the ability to make a woman want him for himself alone.

He turned abruptly, started to walk away, then turned and faced her again.

'Don't be too sure that I can't have a woman any other way!' His voice was a low growl. 'Nor that I think so little of your own standards that I would attempt to seduce you for the price of a Mercedes — '

Her mind reeled. But she knew she hadn't misunderstood him. 'You said, only a moment ago, that I needn't — '

'I seem to have said too much this evening. I let myself be carried away, and spoke without thinking. But if my senseless words gave you the impression that I entertained such a crude thought, then obviously we don't have a rapport between us after all.' His long legs took him to the entry way in moments. 'Good night.'

The door made a small slam as he went out, and Ginger's fury mounted. She wanted to have the last word herself. Her mind was boiling over with insults to his character and his perception of hers. Seconds lengthened into minutes while she rehearsed all the invectives she would have heaped on him, had he not withdrawn from the battle like a coward.

She ran into her bedroom and yanked off her clothes, all the while remembering every word they'd said. Slowly, rational thinking returned. Embarrassment edged its way inside her mind. She'd obviously leaped to a false conclusion. She'd imagined an insult where none existed. How could she have been so stupid, so impulsively wrong? She caught a glimpse of herself in the mirror, her hair tousled and wild. She'd been too defensive again, too impetuous. If they weren't careful, the temper that went with their red hair was going to lead to more explosive scenes. Then she corrected herself. There would be no future scenes. She would never see him again.

6

Not even his six-block walk in the cold breeze off the ocean could cool Neil's anger and the fevered flush on his face. What a fool he'd been to try to make love to Ginger Maddox. Yes, she was the most exciting woman he had met in California; but he should never have given in to temptation. Worse, he had apparently said something stupid and nearly ruined everything. For the good of his mission, he must somehow win back her trust. As to whether he could ever win the woman herself, only time would tell.

★   ★   ★

All day Sunday Ginger rehearsed how she would approach Neil and exactly what she would say. She had been indescribably rude to him, accused him of trying to seduce her in exchange for her broker's commission, insulted him. The mere thought of what she'd said made her face hot and her stomach twist. She knew that the first thing was for her to apologize to Neil. Actually that was the easy part.

After that, somehow she had to let him know, without seeming petty or irresponsible, that she could no longer handle his stock transactions at Benson, Field and Smith.

In her office on Monday morning, she went over all of it in her mind again. The steady hum of voices — punctuated occasionally by the distant peal of a telephone bell — went unnoticed. She stared blankly at the wall of her office and idly fingered the edges of *Barron's Weekly* on her desk, unable to concentrate on anything except the confrontation with the man who had so stirred her that even thinking about him caused an almost unbearable tenseness in her body.

But did it need to be a confrontation?

She could simply drop him a note and inform him she would turn over his account to another representative. No, she corrected herself: that was too cowardly to be considered. A phone call, perhaps. She could be calm and professional on the telephone, actually a large part of her job. But her conscience refused that solution too.

Her mind and body were at opposite poles this morning, her brain telling her she must do the right thing, and her body postponing the decision.

She rehearsed her speech to him for the hundredth time. She really must do it that very minute. Soon her phone would ring with orders to execute; she had other clients, after all. The choice to pick up the telephone and dial his number won out. She lifted the receiver.

'Good morning.' The telephone did not bring the deep resonant voice of Neil Cameron to her, instead he walked into her office and said the words in person. He deposited himself in the walnut chair, his face a mask hiding feelings she suddenly wished desperately to know.

She told the receptionist to hold her calls, then replaced the instrument, never taking her gaze from his face.

Before he spoke again, the frown creasing his forehead disappeared. As if looking at her had somehow dissipated his anger, the muscles around his mouth relaxed. A hint of laughter softened his voice.

'No 'good morning' in return? You were much friendlier Saturday night. Well, up to a point.'

Ginger found her voice at last. 'A point you have every right to remember with distaste.' She hurried along, anxious to say her speech before she could stop herself.

'I'm so terribly sorry for what I said the other night. It was not only wrong, but stupid of me to assume — I mean, please forgive me.'

She let out her breath and dropped her gaze to her lap.

'I'm touched by your apology,' he said, 'but I shouldn't have brought up the matter in the first place.'

'No, you were right to remind me. Although I was prepared to call you if you hadn't shown up just now.'

'If I were a gentleman, I wouldn't have been quite so — shall we say *amorous* to begin with. You had warned me, after all, that friendship was as far as our relationship was likely to go. I plead guilty to letting the firelight and your beauty get the better of me.'

He was apologizing to *her*. Ginger searched his face for some sign he might be teasing her; but he seemed perfectly sincere.

'As I was making my way here,' he went on, 'I was planning to tell you that I'm taking my business elsewhere. But after a walk in the damp air you people call 'morning mist' I've changed my mind. As I said, what happened Saturday night was entirely my fault, and I take full responsibility.' He paused and his warm brown eyes seemed to linger over her face.

Ginger opened her mouth to answer, but he continued before she had an opportunity to say anything.

'I'm used to having my own way, but there's something about you that gives me mixed emotions. Damn it!' he exploded suddenly, although his voice was intense rather than loud, 'I have no intention of apologizing for trying to make love to you. I'd do it again in a minute. But I shouldn't have given in to those feelings. Furthermore, some of the things I said were out of line. I'm afraid I spoke in the heat of the moment and I must have hurt you deeply.'

Ginger managed to cut in at this point. 'Please, don't say any more. I don't want to talk about Saturday night. We've each apologized and, as far as I'm concerned, the matter is closed.'

Neil grinned, grasped her hand and squeezed it, but she quickly pulled it away and began her speech.

'You're not the only one to think that

it's best for both of us if we don't work together in the future. I've decided to turn your account over to John Benson. He's the son of the founder. You'll find him an excellent broker.'

There, she'd said it. It hadn't been so hard after all. But then, why did her heart still pound as if wanting to escape from her chest, and why did her eyes sting so that she felt she might cry? She took a deep breath and regained control.

The sounds of the large office surrounding her cubicle suddenly lessened, making the halt in their conversation uncomfortably obvious. Ginger shifted uneasily in her chair, smoothed the edges of her pink jacket where it rested against the matching skirt, and looked at her desk, rather than his face.

He became businesslike again, his voice taking on a brisk tone. 'As I've said, I considered that alternative, but decided it was not only cowardly, but not in my best financial interests. I don't want anyone else handling my account. I respect your judgment and I want to continue working with you. For my part, I promise never to try to take advantage of you again.'

Ginger's eyes continued to burn, and the butterflies in her stomach swarmed again. She lifted her gaze to his eyes once more and saw a look that told her more than he perhaps realized. Had it been so very difficult for him to make that speech? How much better it would be for both of them if they simply ended their relationship now, before either of them was badly hurt. But he apparently didn't want that.

'Thank you.' Her voice dropped. 'I appreciate the compliment, but I'm afraid it's impossible for us to continue working together under the circumstances.'

'Then you admit the attraction between us.' His inflection rose, his voice taking on an eager tone.

'I don't see how I could deny it. But that doesn't mean I approve.'

'Approve?' he repeated. 'Since when

do we approve or disapprove our emotions? They happen and if we're smart we go where they lead us.'

'No,' she countered, 'if we're smart we weigh the consequences and make sensible decisions.'

'I've agreed not to touch you again, but I don't see why we can't be more than friends. We're both unattached; there's no harm in letting things happen as they will.'

'Not to you, perhaps. Aside from the ethics of the matter, I have no intention of getting involved with anyone.'

'You offered friendship the other night. Isn't that a kind of involvement? Why do you want to withdraw that?'

'I'm afraid I was being naive.' She struggled to find words to make him understand. 'Look, you know the broker-client relationship is a special one. If the two parties become romantically attached, all kinds of problems can arise. Ethics problems. I could be accused of treating you differently from other clients, giving you special favors.

You could be accused of pressuring me for privileged information — '

'I would never do that,' he insisted.

'And I believe you, but that's not the point. What matters is others' perception. Brokers, like Caesar's wife, must be above suspicion.'

He was silent, his forehead wearing a frown, and she reached into her drawer and removed his thin, new-looking folder. She would hand it over to John Benson right away and be done with it. She got to her feet and rounded the corner of her desk.

He stood at almost the same moment and one strong hand caught hers, bringing her close to him. Her gaze flew to his face, where she saw his earlier expression had been replaced by a fierce determination. She could easily believe he usually got his own way. And perhaps she had revealed too much about her own vulnerability by letting him know she doubted she could keep their relationship on a friendly basis. But she straightened her shoulders and firmed her mouth. She was known for getting her way as well, and that day would see the end of their association.

'Don't be hasty,' he said. 'As long as we're not 'romantically attached,' as you put it, no one can find fault with friends doing business. We can still work this out.'

'I don't think so. You may be willing to continue to run the risk of further problems — problems that will only end with pain for one or both of us — but I'm not. I know what I want.'

His fingers circled her slender wrist and the pressure brought her arm down to her side. With his other hand he removed the folder from her grip and placed it on the desk, all the while staring into her face, his lips slightly parted, ready to speak. Their bodies were within inches of touching, and Ginger wondered if anyone else in the office had glanced up, when their heads appeared above the partition, and was watching the drama they were playing out, wondered why they stood so close together.

The moment passed and, after leading her back to her chair, he relaxed his hold and sat down. She did the same. Although his gesture merely postponed the inevitable, she was grateful they were no longer in view. She didn't want a scene.

'The investment I made last week,' he began, as if he had found the solution to the problem, 'was a very small part of what I intend to bring to your firm.' He leaned forward across the desk. 'I'm talking about real money, a lot of it.'

Ginger felt almost threatened by the tone in his voice. Was he bribing her again, subtly suggesting she would lose out on huge commissions if she relinquished his account? If so, he was going to fail. Yes, it would be nice to see larger commissions, but not at the cost of abandoning common sense. The long hours of Sunday, when she had debated with herself about this man, had ended with the right decision. No amount of money would convince her to continue seeing him and risk stirring that up again.

As much as her temper wanted release, she restrained herself, breathed deeply and collected her thoughts. 'Money has nothing to do with this. You said Saturday night that we had no rapport between us after all, and I agree with you. You can't change my mind by dangling large commissions in front of me.'

'You're misjudging me again.' His words came slowly, as if he weighed every one of them. 'I'm not talking about commissions either. I'm speaking of loyalty to your firm, fair play.'

She frowned. 'What does loyalty have to do with it?'

He leaned back in his chair, elbows on the arms of it, making a tent of his long fingers. 'You offer me John Benson. I counter offer with Merrill Lynch.'

'Merrill Lynch? What do you mean?' But even before he replied, the answer came into her thoughts: he intended to take his business out of the firm, to a competitor.

'I don't think they'll have any qualms about handling my account,' he said offhandedly. 'Our association could be one of instant rapport.' He looked triumphant.

Ginger slumped in the chair, unconsciously biting her lower lip while her thoughts swirled. It had never occurred to her that he would take his business down the street. There was more than her feelings for him at stake now. What would her boss think if she allowed such a lucrative account to leave the firm? A fiery sensation stole across her cheeks. How could she ever explain to Jim Blake the poor way in which she had repaid his confidence in her?

7

Eyes narrowed, Ginger stared back at Neil and saw a tiny, devilish grin turn up the corners of his lips. He knew he had her in a bind. Worse, he seemed to be enjoying it. Trapped, she saw no alternative but to surrender. Turning her head from side to side, she signaled 'no,' but her words acknowledged defeat.

'You make it very difficult, Mr. Cameron.'

'So we're back to Mr. Cameron, are we? Well, Ms. Maddox, I can accept that.' He leaned forward again, eyes searching hers, his voice soft and cajoling. 'I'm not really an enemy, you know. Jim Blake has only the highest praise for your work and my aunts insisted I contact you.' He held out his hands like a supplicant. 'I know when I'm well off.' He grinned. 'And, if you want to be formal, I'll be formal. Whatever is necessary. Just continue to handle my account. Please.'

It was the *please* that did it. That such a wealthy and powerful man had pushed aside his ego to that extent humbled her. Who was she to deny him the opportunity to make up for what he considered his bad behavior? If he was certain he could keep their relationship on a friendly basis, couldn't she at least try to do the same? Yes, from now on she would be the consummate professional and not let her feelings get in the way of her work.

'Very well,' she said, straightening her back, 'I'll continue to handle your account, at least temporarily.'

'That's better.'

'But I intend to keep you to your promise. There will be nothing of a personal nature between us and you will not touch me again. Is that understood?'

'Perfectly. Shall we shake on it?' He extended his hand across the desk, and for a moment, Ginger, in an automatic reaction, almost put hers into it. She stopped.

He laughed. 'That was unfair, but I couldn't resist.'

She almost laughed herself at the trick he'd tried to play on her. And, it made her relax. 'Let's get down to business.'

'If that's what you want.'

'Just one more thing,' Ginger added. 'There will be no more secrets between us. At the moment you have me at a disadvantage, because I can't let my personal feelings come before the good of the firm. But I'll change my mind in an instant if I think anything under-handed is going on.'

He didn't answer and she went on. 'First of all, I want to know exactly what it is that you do. Your application indicated you work for the market newsletter called 'Good Times.' Do you invest for them?'

'No, I'm a private investor. But recently I joined the staff of the newsletter put out by Ned Weiser, and we're planning to open a branch office here in San Francisco.'

The name Ned Weiser sounded vaguely familiar to Ginger, but exactly where she had heard it before eluded her. 'I'm afraid I haven't heard of your newsletter.'

'It's new,' Neil explained. 'Weiser worked in the research department of a bank before he decided to publish it. He's only been in business for a year, but he's already making a profit and his predictions have been remarkably accurate.'

'That's impressive,' Ginger admitted. 'I understood most don't make money for several years. What's the purpose, though, of opening a second office?'

'That was my idea. I thought having an office on the west coast might be an advantage. Actually, I'm on my own in this venture. I get market recommendations from Weiser to pass on to his newsletter clients, but making the office pay for itself will be my responsibility.'

'I wish you luck. What about your trades?'

'My trades will not be connected in any way with the newsletter. They will be strictly my own. 'Good Times' does not trade, it merely gives advice to others.'

'I see.'

'It's not that it's unethical, or anything, you understand, that's just the way we want it.'

'I know it's not unethical. I also know it's relatively easy to start one, but usually difficult to make it pay. Between hiring people for research and advertising to get subscribers — '

'Right. You register with the Securities and Exchange Commission, fill out a form that you've never been convicted of a felony and, as long as you don't handle other people's money, that's all there is to it.'

'It's really too easy.'

Neil smiled and again the attraction to him welled up in her, threatening her composure.

'I agree,' he said. 'Of course, some people cut overhead by doing it all themselves or with relatives. I suppose you've heard the story about the newsletter started some years ago by a young man who hawked them on Wall Street for fifty cents each.'

A broad grin replaced the smile, and Ginger could see that Neil loved telling the tale the way some people enjoyed coming to the punch line of a good joke. 'He had an old ditto machine in the basement and his mother collated them on her kitchen table. He was sixteen years old.' He paused. 'The S.E.C. form didn't ask his age.'

Ginger couldn't help laughing. 'What a wonderful story.'

'You know San Francisco stories. I know lots of stories about Wall Street. I'll tell you more some day.'

Some day. There it was again, his intimating that they would spend time together outside of the office, even though they'd just promised each other to stick strictly to business. Suddenly she wished they were away from it this very moment. She regretted they couldn't be friends. Experience had already proved that her attraction to the man was dangerous, but somehow she had to remain professional. She brought herself quickly back to their earlier subject.

'That explains who you are,' she said, and paused, realizing it actually did no such thing: there were dozens of other questions she would like to ask about him. 'But doesn't explain the relationship between you and Harlan Taylor, why you pretended no interest in Taylor Technology stock, when all the while you and he are apparently good friends.'

Once more Neil leaned back in his chair, stretching his legs forward. 'I'll answer you as truthfully as I can.'

'What does *that* mean?'

He ignored her question and went on. 'You made a perfectly valid assessment of Taylor Technology. Their earnings look good and their stock will rise. But not much longer.'

'Is this a market tip from Ned Weiser?'

He paused, deep in thought, for several seconds. 'Yes and no. The point is the rise occurred for reasons other than those you gave. They've been the object of a takeover attempt.'

Ginger's eyes widened and her thoughts flashed to some of the articles she had read about the company. 'Of course,' she began, 'any well-managed company can be considered for a takeover. But, in this case, I haven't heard any rumors to that effect. Do you know who's interested?'

'The offer to buy Taylor has been withdrawn,' he said, not answering her question. 'The point is, I knew that when that happened, the stock price would drop again.'

'But you did buy it.'

'You talked me into it. Is that so hard to understand? And your offer was irresistible.' He was grinning at her again.

Ginger felt uncomfortable, remembering that rash boast of the week before, and, more important, her leaping to the conclusion, Saturday night, that he wanted to make love to her in exchange for it. In the colder light of day, she knew she'd been mistaken about his intentions and she had apologized for accusing him, but his own apology indicated he, too, had played a part in their misunderstanding.

'So I'd like to close out my position in the stock,' he said. 'That will take care of both my ambivalent feelings and the matter of the commission you promised to repay.'

She turned to the computer terminal and punched in the symbol of the stock. 'Thirty and seven-eighths,' she read. 'It's higher, so you've made a profit after all.'

'And you don't have to give up the commission.'

Something about the tone in his voice almost weakened her resolve. If her offer had been irresistible, then what about him, his touch, his kisses? She had to forget those moments in his arms, moments that could never be repeated. She would stop thinking about this provocative man.

Pushing aside the newspaper on her desk, she filled out the paperwork for the sale of the stock. Suddenly another disturbing thought flooded in. She looked up at Neil again.

'How do you know the takeover offer was withdrawn?'

'I have my sources.'

Ginger felt annoyance intrude. He was simply too mysterious. 'Did Harlan Taylor encourage the takeover?'

'Certainly not. Would you want *your* company taken over?' He gazed at her so intently that her annoyance melted, and instead she felt a warmth creep up her neck and spread across her cheeks.

'That all depends, I suppose,' she said, managing to speak in a normal tone.

'Well, in Harlan's case, since he started the business himself, and it bears his name, I can't see how he could be happy at the prospect of someone else having a controlling interest and telling him how to run it.'

Ginger thought that over. She could almost hear the pride in Neil's voice as he described his friend's achievement. At the same time, she could imagine the situation from the point of view of someone who felt helpless under circumstances he could not easily change. On one hand, the price of a stock usually rose dramatically on takeover rumors, making the owner, and anyone else who held it, immeasurably wealthier. With the offer withdrawn, however, the price just as abruptly dropped, leaving everyone with vastly diminished holdings. It was a two-edged sword and could lead to a serious dilemma in the mind of a company officer. Depending on the circumstances, this could be considered insider information. And acting on insider information was not only unethical, it was illegal.

'Just where did Ned Weiser get the information that Taylor might be a candidate for a takeover?'

'Did I say that it had been Weiser?'

'You said 'yes and no' when I asked you.'

He seemed to know her thoughts. 'If you mean did he have insider information, I'm afraid I can't answer that. All I know is that *I* didn't have any insider information. By the time items are published in the newsletter, they're already well known.'

Ginger became instantly on guard again. He sounded evasive. 'This one wasn't, not to me, at any rate. And I'm hardly uninformed.'

Neil paused, his eyes searching hers as if for a sign of understanding. 'What can I say except, trust me?'

Ginger questioned her reactions. Had she been too suspicious? What qualities in this man seemed to produce those feelings? Or was it a straw she grasped to keep from succumbing to his obvious charm?

'I think that concludes our business today,' she said.

'Unless you want to suggest something else for me to buy.' His words were accompanied by a conspiratorial smile that reminded her of her previous recommendation and rash promise. He leaned forward again, eyes darting over her hair, her face, her throat.

A warning flutter began inside, and she wished he would end their interview quickly before her resolve began to slip. His look alone brought sensations that made a mockery of her determination to ignore the man. 'I'm afraid not,' she said. He had asked for her trust and, on an impulse, she decided to give it, but nothing more, not now.

'Actually, I'm not ready to buy anything more today, but perhaps you'd keep an eye on First Continental Insurance Company for me. I'd be grateful for your opinion of it.'

Ginger frowned. Wasn't that the same insurance company whose stock his aunts had asked her to buy for them the week before? She started to comment on the coincidence, then remembered the emphasis the ladies had placed on the confidentiality of the account. Again, the mystery that seemed to surround Neil surfaced. She tried to be realistic. He had explained his strange behavior over Taylor and why he came to San Francisco. As for the stock, what difference did it make that he and his aunts were both interested in the same company? Either he had given them the suggestion or they had given it to him.

'I'd be glad to,' she murmured, and again turned to the terminal for the most recent quote. 'It's forty-five today. I'm not very knowledgeable about the company, but I'll be glad to check with our research department.'

'Fine.' Neil picked up his copy of the sell order and his hand brushed hers briefly over the cluttered desk.

Ginger pulled hers away quickly, before she could fully enjoy his touch. She stood up, a signal ending their business for the day. Neil rose too and again stretched his hand forward.

This time, Ginger, anticipating it, didn't move.

He laughed. Then his eyes searched her face, as if looking for more than she wanted to show. She remembered his caresses, and the searing heat of that moment in her apartment returned again, driving like a burning poker into the center of her being.

'I've agreed to stay friends, Ginger,' he said, his voice seductive, 'but some day you'll want us to be more than that.' He paused. 'You will, you know.'

8

Sunday was the last day in the week Ginger would have expected to see Neil. That afternoon she stopped at a flower stall and bought some lilies to brighten her apartment. Then, as she began to walk back, she suddenly saw him across the street. How had he come to be in that particular neighborhood?

When she reached the corner, he saw her and hurried across to join her on the sidewalk. 'What a nice surprise.'

'If you had a feather handy,' she said, 'you could knock me over with it.'

'Same here. I didn't expect to see you.' He glanced back at the flower stall, which looked like a miniature cable car, and she followed his gaze as it flickered over the colorful blossoms.

'Really?' Considering the other times he had turned up when she least expected him, it wasn't too far-fetched to imagine that he'd put his spies to work to learn her habits.

'Scout's honor,' he said. 'But we both live in this area, so I guess it's not that surprising after all.'

Perhaps not, but the difficult part was figuring out whether she was happy or sad about it. Her rapidly beating heart gave a clue that, once again, she was glad to see him, regardless of whether or not that was prudent.

She turned and continued her journey. 'I thought you were going to buy a condo in Jim Blake's building?'

'Not my type after all. I'm renting a flat in an old Victorian like yours.'

So in a way she'd been right. At least he'd rented an apartment near hers. But he didn't give her time to think about it. He took her arm and walked her rapidly to the next corner.

'But it's wonderful to see you, and I need your help.'

'What kind of help?'

'I need office space and I'm on my way to check out a place now. Come with me, won't you? I'd like your opinion.'

'I don't think my opinion of an office would be very valuable.'

'Then come with me just to keep me company. Sundays are such lonely days when you're a stranger in town.'

His eyes beseeched her and she felt herself melting. What had happened to all her resolve to avoid being alone with him? Yes, she was terribly attracted to him, but she knew that mustn't go anywhere as long as they did business together. Furthermore, she didn't want a relationship with another man. No one could really take Colin's place in her heart.

On the other side, however, was the fact that, if he was telling the truth, he was both lonely and a neighbor. All he wanted was a little of her time, in daylight and in public. There was no danger. How could she refuse?

Ten minutes later, they were on a cable car on California Street and he had changed the subject.

'Why do you have this fixation about money?' he asked. 'For a woman in your profession, that seems a contradiction.'

'It is and I don't,' Ginger protested. They were standing on the outside step and, as the cable car reached the cross street and leveled out, she took a firmer hold with her free hand before the car once more descended the slanting street. 'I leave that to some of my clients!'

Neil placed his right arm around her waist. Although she stiffened momentarily at the intimacy, she permitted it to remain there. With the cable car making its swift descent, his touch gave her a feeling of security. A week had passed since their last encounter, and she had become more confident of her ability to remain friends.

'Maybe you don't realize it,' he persisted.

'What are you,' she asked, turning to look into his face, 'a psychiatrist? Are you going to analyze me here and now?'

Her light tone contrasted with her words.

He laughed softly. 'I have only amateur standing, I'm afraid. When I dated Darlene — I mean Darryl — I often sat in the empty theater during her rehearsals and listened to the director, a staunch disciple of the Stanislavsky method, tell the cast members about motivation for their lines.'

'Darryl must have been good at motivation.'

'Not quite good enough. Perhaps if she had been, she would have realized our marriage couldn't work.'

'What has this to do with me and my so-called fixation about money?' Ginger said, bringing him back to the subject. She didn't mind his talking about his former wife since she felt no jealousy. How could she, when she knew her relationship with Neil would remain strictly business, always?

He paused while the cable car gripman rang the bell, its clang effectively cutting off conversation among passengers for several seconds. 'I meant I learned a lot in those days about why people react in certain ways. In your case, although you deal in money every day, I suspect you don't really like it.'

Ginger thought carefully before answering. 'I don't like or dislike money, per se. I like what it seems to do for the quality of life.' She grinned at him. 'Someone once said, 'Money isn't everything, but — ''

'' — it sure beats whatever's in second place,'' Neil finished for her.

'I wasn't quoting that one,' Ginger said, laughing. 'I meant, 'money may not buy happiness but it makes misery easier to bear.''

Neil smiled broadly. 'I like that too. Say, wait a minute,' he added, pretending to be annoyed, 'you were supposed to let me tell the Wall Street stories, while you told the ones about San Francisco.'

'A quotation about money isn't necessarily about Wall Street.' She smiled. 'Everyone knows old jokes.'

'You're still trying to change the subject.'

'Not really. I just meant that money isn't terribly important to me — I can take it or leave it — although I certainly appreciate that a certain amount of it makes my life more comfortable than it might otherwise be.' She glanced down at her ice-blue pant suit from Saks. Would she be just as happy to shop at a discount store for her clothes?

'Here's our stop,' Neil interrupted, and the car halted. He took her elbow and helped her down.

Ginger welcomed the conversation's end. Perhaps when it resumed, it would be on a different topic, like the errand they were on today.

As they skirted the Embarcadero, she said, 'I wasn't aware of office space in this area. And will they be open on Sunday?'

'There is some, but we're going to Sausalito, and, yes, the man I spoke to said he'd be there to show it.' They had reached the Ferry Building, and he purchased two tickets on the ferry.

'Sausalito?' She grinned. 'Don't you think that's a bit remote from the financial district?'

'I've already explained I like Marin County.'

She shrugged. 'Well, it's your office. In all honesty, I suppose ferrying to work every day has its attractions.'

'I might live over there too,' he added, 'and since I'll spend most of my time on the telephone, anyway, where I do it isn't all that important.'

They waited with scores of other people before boarding. The bay was as blue as the sky, and a breeze put tiny caps of white on the gentle waves and swirled Ginger's hair. A few puffy white clouds made a picture-postcard look of the scene, perfected by Neil's handsome appearance.

'Go on,' he urged, as they found seats on the upper deck and the ferry moved slowly out into the bay. 'You were telling me how you felt about money.'

'I can't get you off this subject, can I?' Ginger sighed slightly, trying to think of something to say that would not be evasive, yet manage to satisfy his curiosity. 'I confess I enjoy some of the good things in life, but my parents weren't rich and I don't know if I could adjust to real wealth.' She looked away toward the East Bay hills, letting the cool breeze fan her cheeks, wondering if he had another motive for his questions.

'But many of your clients must be very wealthy. Doesn't that give you any ideas?'

'Not really.' She paused and then something she had not thought of in years came to mind. 'I once had a very wealthy uncle — a great-uncle, actually — and when the stock market crashed in 1929 he killed himself.'

'A window-jumper,' Neil said, then quickly added, 'I'm sorry. I didn't mean to sound flip about it.'

'That's all right. I never knew him. It happened long before I was born. He didn't jump from a window, though. Actually, those stories were greatly exaggerated. As the Wall Street story expert, you should know that.'

'Another myth shot to pieces,' he said, pretending dismay. Seriousness returned almost at once. 'But you do invest for yourself, don't you, not just for others?'

'Oh, I have some shares of my own, safe things, the kind that widows and orphans are always urged to buy.' The word 'widows' struck her forcibly. She was a widow. How strange the word sounded, as if she were some elderly white-haired woman, not the person who sat with Neil in the noon sunshine.

As if reading her thoughts, his hand stole over hers where it rested on the wooden bench seat. She felt the warm strength of it and didn't pull away. But he expected more of an answer from her. As her eyes roamed over the cityscape passing by on their port side, she sorted out her motivations.

'Because of my uncle's experience,

and the way family members talked about the tragedy, I learned a lot. I don't believe in pinning ones hopes and dreams to great wealth. Unlike Uncle Richard, I would never care so much about money that I would die because I lost any. On the other hand, going into the brokerage business was not a carefully thought-out decision. It just sort of happened.'

'Because of your husband, you mean?'

'Yes.'

'But were you attracted because of his interest in money?'

'I think you're struggling to put Freudian touches into this,' Ginger said. 'Like most undergraduates at the time, our sole interest in money concerned whether we could persuade our parents to send enough to keep us in hamburgers and movies on Saturday night.'

'But Colin majored in Business and then you joined him. Instead of Library Science.'

'You have a good memory,' she said, returning her gaze to his suntanned face.

'I remember everything about you.' His voice dropped to a whisper. 'I remember the taste of your mouth.'

'Don't!' She pulled her hand away from his. Perhaps it was a mistake to come with him. If he reminded her of the way she had responded to his kiss, or anything else that occurred that evening, she'd regret her decision.

She tried to change the subject. 'We're doing entirely too much talking about me.'

'I'm still trying to figure out why you ended up a broker, that's all.' He shifted on the bench, moving closer to her.

'I've told you. When Colin was killed, Jim Blake suggested I come into the firm. I went to school for three months and here I am. Although I could never be fanatic about money, that doesn't mean I can't handle stock transactions efficiently.'

Neil paused, looking at her through narrowed eyes, before speaking. 'Yes, I agree. I think that answers my question. There's only one more.'

'Good! And that is — ?'

'Do you ever regret not going back into Library Science?'

'Not really. Frankly, I think I might have been bored with it. Sometimes things work out better for us accidentally than if we had given them previous thought.'

'I disagree. For real happiness, I think we need to define our goals and then go where they can be fulfilled.' One hand went across the back of the bench and he leaned toward her.

She turned her head away from his penetrating look. 'After marrying Colin, my own career in business became my goal. In spite of a degree, though, I started out in public relations at a canning company. Then I worked my way up to executive assistant to a vice president.'

'That's impressive.'

'Not really. For 'assistant,' read 'secretary,' and you'll understand. I soon learned it was a dead end.' The memory of that bitter realization returned, making her eyes narrow and jaw tighten. 'I could never become anything higher or be made an officer of the company.' After a slight pause, she let herself relax. The past was over. 'So, when Colin was killed and Jim offered me the opportunity to take his place, I jumped at it. I haven't regretted the decision.'

'Since I'm fascinated by the stock market myself, I can certainly understand that, but did you ever think about fighting for your rights at the canning company?' His hand reached for hers again. 'Perhaps you could have had them up before the E.E.O.C. You seem like a fighter to me.'

'Believe me, I tried everything short of that. Yes, they were in violation of the 'Equal Opportunity' laws, but it would have been a hollow victory at best. I liked the people I worked with. It was the system that needed changing. And if I had fought them and won a promotion, I would have had to face a lot of angry people. The job wouldn't have given me pleasure anymore.'

His voice turned from earnest to tender. 'But it mustn't be pleasant to work in the same place that Colin did, to be reminded of him every day.'

He had struck at her very soul, it seemed, but she didn't flinch. She had accepted that challenge and resolved it. 'Strangely, it's a comfort. I wouldn't have thought so at first, but there's a kind of feeling of being close to him. I don't expect you to understand.'

'I think I do.' His fingers made gentle circles on her arm.

She thrust her hands into her jacket pocket. She felt too fully revealed to this man who remained, in many respects, a total stranger. 'Please,' she said. 'Let's change the subject. You're examining me like a specimen under a magnifying glass. I came with you today to help you find an office. Let's concentrate on that for awhile.'

'I'm sorry. I've overstepped the bounds again, and I have no right to pry into your personal life. But I find people endlessly fascinating. You especially.'

'Then don't! I didn't want to continue our — our relationship, but you insisted. So we're going to be just friends, remember?'

'You're right.' He stood up and rested the small of his back against the ferry railing at their side. 'I'll stick to business for the rest of the day. Just smile at me once more, please.'

His look cajoled, like a small boy asking for a treat, and her sternness melted. A tiny smile pulled at her lips. 'All right.'

Smiling too, he continued to study her profile, and Ginger looked out at the passing scenery.

She wondered why he had asked so many questions about her attitude toward money, almost as if he were investigating her like a bond company.

He might be her wealthiest client. Was he hinting she should become interested in him because of that? Or, since she knew a lot about his finances, was he worried she'd like him only for his money? But no: they'd already settled that matter. It was *she* who kept insisting they were just friends. And what about his own interest in finance? In spite of his curiosity about her, she wouldn't ask him. She didn't want to know about his personal life, except for what he volunteered. It was a kind of balancing act, making sure he would keep his distance.

She stood up and leaned forward against the railing, watching the wake of the boat ripple outward and the gulls swoop and dive. As the vessel edged into its berth on the Marin County side, he said, 'Let's visit the shops first.'

'Are you sure you have some offices to inspect over here?' Ginger asked, her suspicions returning.

'One,' he said, 'I found it in the newspaper classified section. But I'm early for my appointment, so we have some time to kill.' With that he took her arm and helped her down the steps to the main deck, and they stepped onto the wooden gangway.

They crossed the street and went into a souvenir shop. Tourist items filled every shelf: trays and glasses with pictures of the Golden Gate Bridge painted on them, plastic place mats, tee shirts, kites, and dozens of knickknacks. They spent little time there, bought nothing, and finally found a taxi to take them to the address of a building which had a vacant office on its second floor.

A quick look, guided by a short, middle-aged Italian who spoke with a heavy accent, convinced Neil it was unsuitable, and he thanked the man before they hurried out to the sidewalk.

As they stood there for a few minutes, Ginger couldn't help teasing. 'But you like this side of the bridge, remember?'

'Don't rub it in,' he said, feigning displeasure. 'I'm willing to admit you were right when you said the city might be a better place to look. Still,' he added, smiling down at her, 'I enjoyed the ferry ride, didn't you? And you have to admit this town is charming and picturesque.'

She smiled. 'We agree on that at least.' As they strolled back toward the dock, they stopped at an ice cream shop and Neil bought waffle cones for them. They sat on a bench in a nearby park to eat them.

'Would you have dinner with me tonight?' he asked suddenly, leaning back comfortably on the bench.

Ginger thought for a moment before answering. Something inside her wanted to say yes. She felt very much at ease with him by then. Surely the camaraderie could continue without any danger. But almost at once, her imagination pictured the night they had walked to her apartment, sat before the fire. And then — It was the 'and then' she couldn't deal with. She felt able at this moment to resist any future overtures on his part, but why take a chance? Why subject herself to more guilt and remorse?

'No,' she answered finally, with more regret than she cared to admit. She stood up, brushing crumbs from her skirt. 'I don't think that's a good idea. It's getting late. Shall we go?'

He didn't protest, but stood up too and they returned on the next ferry back to San Francisco, again on the upper deck. Neil fed the swooping gulls by throwing bits of leftover waffle into the air; but eventually the birds became bold enough to snatch pieces from his upraised fingers. After they docked, he found a taxi, dropped her at her apartment building and disappeared in the late afternoon traffic.

That evening she fixed a large salad and ate it in front of the television set, watching a documentary about the sinking of the Titanic. She knew she'd done the right thing by refusing to have dinner with Neil, so why did she feel like a passenger on a doomed ocean liner?

9

Ginger had difficulty keeping Neil out of her thoughts, but it was his aunts, the Dillon twins, who called her next. On Wednesday, she lunched with the ladies in the circular tea room in the rotunda of Neiman-Marcus.

'We want to buy some oil stock,' Carrie announced when their lunch arrived and the waitress moved out of earshot.

'Oils look very good right now,' Mary added. 'This new book we just read — '

' — tells all about how to find undervalued stocks,' Carrie continued.

' — and so when we applied the rules, we found — '

' — several oil companies met the criteria.'

'Did you have a particular company in mind,' Ginger asked, 'or do you want me to make a list?' She put down her

140

fork and pulled a small pad and pen from her purse in order to make notes.

'No, dear, that won't be necessary,' Carrie said. 'We've already done that and chosen Standard Oil.'

'Do you mean Exxon?' Ginger asked.

'Of course. I forgot. Mr. Rockefeller was a friend of our grandfather, you see, and old habits die hard.'

'I thought you said you chose it because of a book,' Ginger asked, returning to the earlier remark.

'Of course we did,' Mary said. 'But, when you know someone in the business, well — '

'Grandfather would never forgive us,' Carrie added, 'if we didn't consider someone he was acquainted with — '

Their grandfather was no doubt deceased, and so was Rockefeller, but Ginger decided not to try to find logic in the ladies' choices, and simply wrote the name of the stock. 'How many shares would you like?'

Mary consulted her sister. 'A thousand is enough, don't you think?' The other nodded her head vigorously.

Ginger's eyes widened as she calculated the possible cost of their latest venture into the market. Exxon was selling at about sixty dollars a share, she believed. The ladies seemed not to bat an eye, however, so why should she? She put the paper away and resumed eating her chicken salad.

'Now, about Taylor Technology,' Carrie said, after dabbing at her lips with the edge of her pale pink napkin. 'We want you to sell that — '

Ginger was glad to hear it and wrote on her pad.

' — and sell our First Continental and sell another thousand shares short,' Mary finished.

Ginger's hand stopped midway to the pad. If she had been shocked before, she was dumbfounded then. 'Sell short?'

'Yes, dear. We'll deposit the funds into our account.'

Ginger didn't know which was the more surprising to her: the fact they seemed to know about short selling or their choice of First Continental. Why that company? One moment they seemed like unorthodox neophytes and the next like sophisticated investors. She looked down at her pad again and wrote quickly, but the nagging feeling of something not quite right persisted.

'You do know what selling short means?' she asked. 'It's a procedure in which you — '

'Of course, dear,' Mary said, interrupting her. 'We expect the stock price to drop, and when we cover our short we'll have made a profit.'

'That's true,' Ginger admitted, 'provided the stock really goes down.'

'Oh, we know it will.' Carrie settled back in her chair, a satisfied smile streamlining her mouth.

'You did mention getting ideas from a book, but this is very specific — ' Again Ginger felt that a correct broker-client relationship required that she warn these eighty-five-year-old ladies about a trade that might not be suitable. 'May I ask how you know?'

'That would be telling,' Mary said in a sing-song voice, such as one might use to a child, and wagged her finger sideways. 'We have our own ideas, too, you know.'

'You had me purchase the stock for you only a few weeks ago, and now you want to sell it short. You must admit it's a little puzzling.'

'Of course, dear. But you see,' Carrie said, 'we expect it to go down from now on. We can make money that way too.'

How convenient, Ginger thought, if investing were as simple as that. 'But you must understand,' she pressed, 'that if the stock price goes up instead, you'll be asked to put up more margin. If you own the shares, and they drop, you can never lose more than your original investment. But if you're short and it rises, theoretically — well, the sky's the limit.'

'We know all about that,' Carrie said, a slightly impatient tone in her voice. She sipped her tea again before continuing, 'We don't intend to let that happen to us — '

'We'll be watching,' Mary concluded.

Ginger waited, hoping one of them would volunteer further information, but instead, they changed the subject.

'Mary,' Carrie said to her sister, 'do you have some shopping to do while we're here?'

'Yes, as a matter of fact, I do.'

Feeling dismissed, Ginger swallowed the last of her iced tea, thanked them and left the restaurant. Frustration over the position they had placed her in nagged at her. Yet, perhaps she overreacted because she had come to care about the ladies. They were charming and lovable as well as eccentric. Or was it because she had only recently come into the business? Probably other brokers wouldn't worry for an instant over the peculiarities of their clients.

Still, there were complications, at least in Ginger's opinion. The Dillon sisters' nephew was also her client and he had inquired about First Continental too. Would he also want to sell short? If one client gave information to the other, that would seem to be the next logical step.

Back at her office, she dialed his number and an answering machine took her message. But as soon as she hung up, she regretted her action. The sisters had specifically requested her not to discuss their activities with their nephew. Yet, she had an overriding urge to ask him to explain. Or did she have a private need to speak to him, hear his voice? It was too late to change her mind. She couldn't erase the call. Feeling foolish, she dialed the number again and this time said, 'This is Mrs. Maddox. Please ignore my earlier message.' Then she tried to bury herself in work, so she wouldn't have to wonder what Neil would think about her strange behavior.

She remained in the office later than usual that day, almost expecting him to call back, but finally, telling herself it was better that he hadn't, she went home and prepared her dinner. Later she collapsed in front of the television set where an old movie did its best to occupy her mind. But she found her gaze wandering about the room, noting the soft lines of her quilted Lawson sofa, the antique tables and bookcases that had once belonged to her grandmother. Her living room, not so flashy as Jim Blake's, was more homey, and suited perfectly the converted Victorian house where her apartment constituted the upper floor.

At nine o'clock she got ready for bed, changing into her cranberry-colored nightgown and matching robe. Then her doorbell rang and when she inquired who it was, heard Neil's voice.

'What are you doing here?' Her face got suddenly warm, her heart pounding rapidly in her chest.

'I've come in answer to your summons, Milady.' He sounded playful and jolly.

'I didn't summon you.'

'Two messages on my machine say differently. You need to talk to me, and I certainly need someone to share my nightcap with. Please,' he urged, 'I have something special for us.'

Her curiosity aroused, as only he seemed capable of doing, she pressed the buzzer that unlocked the downstairs door and moments later Neil, with a brown grocery bag in his arms and a very wide, very endearing grin on his face, stood on her threshold. He made a low bow. 'Good evening, Fair Lady.'

She stood aside and let him enter. 'You have a terrible knack of getting your way around me.'

'Wonderful knack,' he corrected, grinning.

'You can come in for a minute, but you can't stay. I don't need to talk to you. I told you that in the second message.'

'All a code, naturally, and I, a student of Hercule Poirot, not to mention the San Francisco detective Sam Spade, have deciphered it. You are thirsty and I am going to make a Raspberry Cameron for you.' With no further invitation, he swept past her and found her kitchen as if he had been there a dozen times instead of once.

She closed her apartment door and followed him, clutching the edges of her robe tightly together and protesting. 'But you can't. It's late and I — '

'You have to get up early. I know. I won't stay long.' He took his purchases out of the bag and placed them on her counter top, never looking directly at her, as if fixing drinks for ladies in their night clothes was nothing to worry about. And he continued talking. 'You'll love this, I promise. I need an ice cream scoop and a sieve, if you have them.'

She found the items while he pulled off his jacket, revealing a short-sleeved polo shirt with an animal embroidered on the pocket. 'Where are your brandy glasses?'

Ginger pointed to a cabinet and then took his coat and placed it on a chair in the other room. When she returned, she found him rinsing a box of fruit in her sink. 'If I can have fresh raspberries like these every week, I shall never leave California.' He placed some of the fruit in the bottom of two of the glasses.

'You seem quite at home,' she commented from the doorway.

'I could get used to it here.' He looked over at her with a smile that did wicked things to Ginger's heartbeat. 'That doesn't mean you just get to stand there. Here, you scoop the sherbet over the raspberries while I open the wine.'

'Oh, I get to help?'

'Of course. Oh, and we need some iced tea spoons too.'

As Neil pulled it from the bottle, the cork made a tiny pop and then he poured the fruity wine over the sherbet. He sprinkled more fresh berries on top and, picking up both glasses, returned to the living room, where he set them on the coffee table. He dimmed her lights, lit the fireplace and placed a glass in her hand. He raised his. 'To friendship.'

She lifted her glass and gently touched his with it. 'I'll drink to that.'

'I thought you would.' He laughed with her, and she realized again how pleasant it was to spend time with him. She wished she knew more about him.

As quickly as the notion came, she thrust it aside. She didn't want to know too much about him, it was dangerous. She must keep their relationship on this light, bantering level.

'It's delicious.' She sat on the extreme left side of the sofa and took another sip. It was refreshingly cool. So why, suddenly, did she feel so warm? Was it the wine? The fire?

'What you're wearing is the exact color of the drink,' he said, as if noticing her robe for the first time. He sat next to her and set his glass back on the coffee table.

'So it is.' She held the drink close to compare the shade and then her hand slipped on the frosty sides of the glass and it tilted. Wine splashed forward out of the glass, over her robe and into her lap, forming a small pool.

Both of them erupted into motion. Neil took her glass and slammed it down carelessly on the table, then whipped a handkerchief from his pocket and attempted to wipe at the spill. Ginger automatically jumped to her feet and began to pull the wet garment from her shoulders. Only when it lay in a heap at their feet did she realize she stood before him clad only in her nightgown, its lacy top, held by thin spaghetti straps, barely covering her upper body.

What had she done? She must get into the other room and change. But her body disobeyed and instead she stood still, mere inches from his waiting arms. They stared at each other.

His voice was a choked whisper. 'I know I promised not to touch you, but does kissing the wine from your body count?'

The firelight danced across his face

and Ginger couldn't speak. The thought of his mouth on her flesh drove every other thought into oblivion. Then, suddenly, it was not Neil whose face loomed in front of her, but Colin.

As quickly as it came, the vision disappeared, but its effect only began after it dissolved. Like an underwater swimmer coming to the surface, she returned to reality. She picked up the robe and clutched it tightly to her body.

'I'm sorry.' Her voice caught and then tears filled her eyes and ran down her cheeks. 'I didn't mean to let this happen. Don't you understand?' The words tumbled out almost inaudibly, as if from another person.

'We're not meant to be merely friends. That's what I understand.' His breathing was ragged.

'I mean — your being here makes me feel as if I'm cheating on Colin.' The words burst from a throat tight with emotion.

He stared at her in silence. Then he reached out and grasped her shoulders, holding her tightly, almost brutally. A look of intense pain crossed his features and his mouth set in a tight line, jaw muscles firm and hard. 'You can't mean that.'

'I'm — ' The moment sharpened, everything became real and painful and full of rules she had made, never to be broken. Her head beginning to clear, she stammered, 'I don't — I mean, I know Colin is dead, but I can't help it.'

Even saying the words wrenched her heart. She had not thought of Colin all evening, but he had suddenly come back to her. His face had come between her and this man to stop her.

'You still feel married to him?'

She could only nod, her breath coming fast and hard, her body beginning to tremble.

She felt him draw a deep, shuddering breath, and his arms dropped away from her. 'I can't fight that,' he said simply, his hands clenched into fists. After a long silence, he spoke again, his voice softer. 'I don't mean to come between you and your memories. I want to build new memories with you, but only if you're willing. Only if it doesn't hurt.'

Ginger saw the compassion written on his features. He knew what it meant to be very hurt. He didn't want to be the one to wound her a second time.

Tears squeezed from her eyelids, her shoulders shook.

He took her in his arms again, held her tightly, the satiny fabric between them, as if he knew he could never hold the real woman again, then let her go.

'Good night.' He headed for the door, grabbing his jacket from the chair as he went. 'Forget this ever happened. It was only a dream.'

She looked at the closed door through eyelashes wet with tears, her body quivering. Was it a dream or a nightmare?

10

The *Wall Street Journal* lay open on Ginger's cluttered desk, but she had read the same article three times and remained no closer to understanding it. Neil's face hovered before her, superimposed on the black printing.

It had been a week since the episode in her apartment, but, if anything, she seemed more aware of the man than ever. When dressing every morning, she chose her most attractive outfit. Often during the day she caught herself looking toward the outer door, expecting him to come in. When she returned to her own apartment and curled up in a chair to read, she found his face and voice intruded on her thoughts and obliterated any attempt at concentration. Colin's face had intruded that night she had once again found herself ready to melt into Neil's arms, but since then, only Neil's features floated before her eyes. Even sleep eluded her while she pondered their relationship.

Why did he affect her so strongly, as no man ever had? Not even Colin had swept her into such a tumult. She loved Colin, had been happy and content with him; but never in their years together had such wild abandon been part of her reaction.

What a remarkable man Neil was. What patience he had shown. How many men would have reacted as he did when she sent him away? Others would have been angry at the very least, would have called her names and stormed out. He had been compassionate, understanding. She felt humbled by the revelation. If she had ever doubted his being the perfect gentleman, she no longer did so. And yet, the dilemma persisted. Even if Colin's vision hadn't appeared, there were still many other problems to consider. However attracted she was to the man, that was something that could never be.

With a sigh, she reached for her cup and realized the coffee was almost stone cold. She rose from her chair, left her small section of the office and headed for the break room upstairs, her feet silent on the dark red carpeting underneath.

As she poured fresh coffee into her cup, Jim Blake entered the room and refilled his own cup.

'Good morning, Ginger, I haven't seen much of you lately, but your weekly totals have improved. At this rate, you'll be top rep for the month. Are you out beating the bushes for business, or have your regular customers decided to invest more?'

'Good morning, Jim. I do have two new customers, but mainly I think it's the increased trading of the Dillon sisters.' Honesty compelled her to admit where the increase had come from, for in truth she felt she had neglected business. Every waking moment seemed to be occupied with thoughts of Neil Cameron.

'What are the ladies up to now?'

Ginger thought of their purchase of Exxon, but more importantly of the short sale in First Continental. A wave of guilt overtook her; she ought to have been more insistent that they not take such a gamble.

'What's the matter?' Jim asked. 'You look worried.'

'Oh, it's nothing I can't handle, but sometimes I do worry about my clients. I want all of them to be successful.'

'So do we all, my dear, so do we all. But let's be realistic. No one wins all the time, either here or at Las Vegas, and those who say they do are either liars or fools.'

'I know that, but — '

'Only one person can buy into a stock at the exact bottom, and only one can sell out at the exact top. And the chances of it being the same person are astronomical. All we can do is hope to go along for a little bit of the ride. If you suggest a stock at a good price, your customer will make some money.'

'I believe everything you're saying, but don't we have a responsibility to keep customers from making terrible mistakes?'

'Of course, and I'm sure you follow that policy, but sometimes we get clients who seem to enjoy defying us.' He frowned. 'The worst part of that is that even though you try to keep them from some folly, which, then, just as you predicted, turns sour, they blame you for it anyway. Then they find another broker, as if he could turn their mistakes into winners.'

'I hope that won't happen in this case,' Ginger said.

He stirred sugar into his cup. 'So do I.'

Suddenly something else occurred to Ginger. 'What do you know about Taylor Technology?'

'Everything you taught me. You did an excellent report on them. So why would I know anything you don't already know?'

'What about rumors? Have you heard

anything of a takeover attempt against them?' She kept her voice even, impersonal.

His lips pinched, he looked away for a moment, deep in thought. 'No — no, nothing of that kind.'

'I hadn't heard anything myself, but in the last week or so, I haven't kept such close tabs on them.' She considered telling Jim that Neil had confided there had been such an attempt, but changed her mind.

'Well,' Jim said, 'Carl Rivvio resigned — he was an officer of the company — but people change jobs every day. Nothing unusual about it that I'm aware of.'

For the second time, a name sounded familiar to Ginger, but she couldn't recall where she'd heard it before.

'Did you read that in the newspaper?'

'I'm not sure. Probably.'

Ginger assumed that's where she'd read it too, but if the name of Taylor Technology appeared in the same article, why hadn't she remembered?

Thanking Jim for his help, Ginger left the coffee room and returned to her office. Despite lack of a good reason, she had a sudden urge to look through her client file and she flipped the Rolodex cards. In the 'R's' she read the name: Carl Rivvio.

An uneasiness stole through her body, like watching a mystery movie and wondering what would happen next. She pulled open the second drawer of her filing cabinet and removed Rivvio's file. She glanced through it, flipping first to the bottom sheet of paper, his application to open the account. The date showed that Colin had filled it out, which explained, perhaps, why the name hadn't been instantly familiar to her.

But the really puzzling thing was that nothing indicated his being an officer at Taylor Technology. Of course, officers weren't necessarily employees. The board of directors could consist of many outsiders. Some individuals did nothing but serve on boards of directors of various corporations.

Her suspicions momentarily calmed, she scanned the copies of transaction forms. The earliest ones were dated almost five years before, and they were for very small amounts. Then came a period of inactivity and finally, just about a year before, a flurry of buy and sell orders, involving large sums of money. Some trades were in Taylor' stock, some were not.

A hunch formed in her mind and she picked up the phone and dialed the offices of Taylor Technology. 'May I speak to Mr. Carl Rivvio, please?'

'I'm sorry,' the receptionist answered, 'he's no longer employed here.'

'I see, but he worked in the — ' She let her intuition guide her. ' — accounting department, didn't he?'

'Yes. Did you want to speak to someone else there?'

'No, thank you.' Ginger hung up. An officer in the accounting department would have first-hand information about financial matters, wouldn't he? Would this information lead to something unethical?

But Ginger had no time to decipher what it all meant, for a tall shadow loomed over her, and Neil entered her office. Her heart pounded. The memories of their recent encounter washed over her like a strong tide.

'Neil.' She paused for a split second to collect her scattered thoughts, wondering if her common sense could override the personal feelings that almost overwhelmed her.

'Good morning.' His smile was bright and open, and his eyes, fringed with thick dark lashes, seemed more hazel than brown. 'You look lovely. Green becomes you.'

Ginger glanced down automatically at her suit made of linen the color of spring leaves. 'Thank you.' Her voice sounded high and squeaky in her ears. Why must he always have this effect on her? Why did his aura of confidence and masculinity ripple outward and engulf her?

She ignored the symptoms and remembered her phone call. 'As a matter of fact, I'm glad you're here.'

His entire face seemed to light up. His eyes sparkled, his mouth widened into an even more devastating smile. He reached across the desk and covered both her hands with his. 'This is more than I dared hope for after last week.'

She pulled free reluctantly. 'This is strictly business.'

His face relaxed and he shrugged. 'It's always either strictly business or strictly friendship between us.'

'What you want between us — ' she began.

He whispered the words. 'Is to have nothing between us, just our bodies doing whatever comes naturally.'

She struggled against the vision he evoked — of him holding her, kissing wine from her body, as he'd suggested — but the memory made inroads on her practicality, and she brought herself back to the subject with difficulty, her face flushed.

'I want to talk about Taylor Technology.'

'What more is there to say? I closed out my position, end of story.' He leaned back in the chair and shifted his legs.

'You told me a few weeks ago about a takeover attempt.'

His eyes took on a wary look. 'It's over now.'

'There never was a takeover,' she accused, her voice low. 'There was an insider scandal and Carl Rivvio resigned.' She looked closely at him to see his reaction to her announcement.

His words came slowly. 'A resignation isn't all that unusual. And there was no scandal.'

'Perhaps not.' Again she spoke in a firm quiet tone. 'I don't believe there ever was a takeover planned, however. I think Rivvio was passing on insider information. And I think someone paid him handsomely for it. What I want to know is who paid him. You?'

The wariness in his eyes turned to

steely hardness. He stared across at her for long moment, then finally seemed to relax again and spoke in low, confidential tones.

'Well, I really wasn't free to tell you about it, but I know I can trust you.'

'Trust me? Don't involve me in anything illegal!' The thought he might made her temples throb.

'Of course not. I took a very small part in it. Anyway, nothing illegal turned up and it's all over.'

'How small a part?' Her curiosity rose now that the mystery seemed near a solution.

'All right, here's the story. You already know that Taylor is a friend of mine from college days.'

'Yes, so you told me.'

'Well, he knew I spent a lot of time on Wall Street, so he called me a few months ago about a problem he had.'

'What kind of problem?'

'He suspected someone was passing on insider information and asked for my help.' He shrugged and became silent again.

Ginger felt he was playing it down, saying as little as possible. 'What could you do from New York? You didn't come to San Francisco until recently.'

'That's right. I didn't do much at all, to tell the truth. I told him what kinds of things to look for. And he did. He found out who it was and the fellow was asked to resign.'

Ginger thought about that for a moment. 'But why did you pretend there had been a takeover attempt?'

'Two reasons. First, Harlan suspected the information being passed on *would* be used in a takeover. Second, it explained the drop that would probably occur in Taylor's stock. Also, I wasn't at liberty to give all the reasons. Harlan imposed restrictions on me to that extent. After all, you can't very well catch a thief if you give him plenty of warning that you suspect him.'

That seemed logical, but Ginger needed still more. 'But it's all over now, you said, so why the continued secrecy?'

'Not secrecy, common sense, Even though Rivvio resigned, it's dangerous to accuse someone. You can be sued for libel.'

'But truth is always the best defense. If he had proof — '

'That's just the point. I don't know exactly what proof Harlan had. Since the press handled it so discreetly, I suspect he didn't have as much as he would have liked.'

Everything Neil said made perfect sense. It had had a simple explanation, after all, and she had been trying to make something mysterious out of it. Relief flooded over her. Only now did she realize she had been almost panic-stricken at the thought that Neil might be involved in something unethical. Strictly business or strictly friendship notwithstanding, she didn't want to think ill of him in even the slightest way. Now she felt more confident that he couldn't possibly be mixed up in anything illegal. She felt the tension ease from her body and let a smile take over her features.

'At least Harlan's business is safe again.' He paused even longer this time. 'Safer than I am.'

She searched his face for the answer to that riddle. 'What do you mean? You're not in any danger, are you?'

'No, I'm only in danger of being miserable because of a certain red-haired lady who causes sleepless nights. And, worst of all, who thinks I might have been guilty of paying off to get insider information.'

Ginger felt her face grow hot. She had unjustly accused him, and of trying to hurt his friend, besides. 'I'm sorry,' she said quickly. 'Really, I am. I just discovered the Rivvio angle this morning and hadn't had a chance to analyze things. It looked as if you were involved somehow, so I just blurted out the first thing that came to my mind. I shouldn't have done that.'

'You're forgiven. It was a natural

reaction, I suppose, since I had given you a little false information in the first place. I should have told you the complete story before, although I didn't know you quite as well as I do now.' His voice had a low rich timbre that made her face feel warm. 'So I'm partly at fault anyway.'

'Don't excuse me completely.' She hastened to take her share of the blame for the misunderstanding. 'I should have thought before speaking. Sometimes I'm too impetuous.'

His eyes swept over her face for some moments before he spoke again. 'You're not the only impetuous one. I realize this isn't the time or place, but I want you to know I understand about the other night. Although I can't promise to stop trying.' He leaned across the desk, bringing his face close to her so she could see tiny strands of silver hair at his temples.

Ginger managed to retain control of her feelings, but merely looking at the curve of his mouth threatened to turn her legs to jelly. 'Please don't say anything. I'm sorry about that too.'

'You have no reason to be.'

She remembered how his lips felt on hers. 'Oh, but I do. And I want you to know how much I appreciate the way you behaved. I — ' She stopped, unable to bring herself to discuss her feelings any more. As she searched desperately for a safer topic of conversation, her telephone rang, rescuing her. Handling an order occupied her for several minutes.

When she turned back to Neil, he looked more business-like. 'I shouldn't be taking up so much of your time.'

'That's all right.' She didn't want him to talk about what happened the other night, but nevertheless felt reluctant to have him leave. 'After all, you are a client. That's what I'm here for, to help you with your investments.' She reached into her desk and pulled out a sheet of paper. 'You asked for more information about First Continental, and this is what the

172

research department has come up with.'

He folded it and thrust it into an inside pocket without a glance. 'Thank you. What's your reaction to the company?'

Ginger was dismayed, partly by his seeming indifference to the report she had gleaned from the research department, and partly because of a guilty feeling that she had not studied the company personally. Except for some superficial knowledge, she had no additional information to offer. She had neglected, along with many other things, to study the company because her thoughts seemed permanently dissuaded from work by the visions of this man himself.

'I'm afraid I don't have anything more to add,' she finished lamely. 'Did you want to buy some stock in the company today?' She almost added, 'or sell,' but that would have been too revealing. Did he know his aunts were short-selling the stock? Should she tell him? Just where did her loyalties lie?

'No, not today.'

Again Ginger felt disappointed. He had insinuated, boasted actually, that he would be doing a lot of trading — 'real money' was the term he used — but so far, he'd done very little. Her thoughts flew back to their discussion of money on the way to Sausalito. He'd been so insistent on finding out her attitude toward it. What about his? What did it mean to him? If he lost it, would it concern him as deeply as it had her Uncle Richard?

Ginger realized she had missed some of Neil's words. 'I'm sorry. What did you say?'

'Not all my funds have been transferred from the East yet. Meantime, thanks for getting the report.' He paused. 'Any chance of your visiting my new office?'

The very thought of it made her heart jump. 'I'd love to.' Her voice sounded perfectly normal, but inside she felt as if a trapped butterfly was trying to escape. And then her conscience spoke up. The visit would take her from her job, and she had too much work to do. Although seeing his office could hardly be construed as a romantic encounter, every moment they were alone together seemed to bring dangerous feelings to the surface. The memory of his seeing her nearly naked body intruded. She swallowed. 'On second thought, I'd better not.'

'Whatever you say.' He looked crestfallen, rose from the chair and went to her office door. 'Maybe some other time.'

She said goodbye and watched him cross the lobby and leave the building. She sighed. She was beginning to get very tired of arguing with herself over this man. When would it end?

11

'It's Friday. Aren't you going to take off a little early today?' Jim Blake had poked his head in Ginger's office, his suit coat over his arm, as if on his way out. Obviously, he was taking his own advice.

'No. I have lots of things to catch up on, paper work that the boss insists on.' She put added emphasis on the final words, but smiled at the same time.

The boss to whom she referred merely shrugged his shoulders. 'Suit yourself. Cynthia and I are going sailing tomorrow. Want to come along?'

Ginger laughed before answering. 'And make a crowd? Not on your life. By the way, have you proposed to the lady yet?'

'Do you think I should do it on the bay? You know, get well heeled over, and perhaps threaten to dump her out if she refuses me?'

Ginger grinned. 'Of course. And with me watching!'

'Well, if you accept, I'll have to ask a man too — '

'Still matchmaking for me?'

' — and then you could propose marriage to him — or vice versa; I'm not particular — while I'm popping the question to Cynthia.'

Again Ginger's unconscious summoned Neil's face and she imagined him proposing to her on board Jim's sailboat, leaning against the railing, the wind ruffling his thick hair, the bright sun crinkling his eyes, and his mouth — For a moment she could almost feel his mouth on hers.

'Well, what do you think?' Jim continued. 'Shall I invite Cameron along too?'

'Jim Blake, you are a devil. Or else he is. What has he told you?' Annoyance grew in Ginger's breast.

'Hold on there. Neil has told me nothing. But one would have to be blind not to see the way he looks at you. He took you home from my party. He's been in the office several times since then, and always to see you.'

'Don't the people in this place have enough work to do to keep them from gossiping about me?'

Jim came fully into her cubicle at that point, settled himself in a chair and lowered his voice significantly. 'The whole office *will* know what's going on if you don't lower your voice.'

Ginger tensed for a moment, then relaxed. 'I'm sorry.'

'You've been like a little sister to me, Ginger. I care what happens to you. Frankly, although I admit I don't know everything about Neil Cameron, I think he would be a good thing to happen to you.'

'No one's going to 'happen to me.' I'm perfectly fine just the way I am. I don't need anyone.' Still, she spoke more forcefully than she had intended, although she was certainly not trying to persuade herself.

'Yes, you do, even though you may not realize it right now. But I have a feeling Neil is willing to wait until then.'

'I don't care what Neil is willing to do. It's what I'm willing to do that counts; and I am *not* going to become involved with him or anyone else.' Even as the words were torn from an old speech she had memorized, she knew they did not represent present reality, and she finished by letting her defiant look dissolve under Jim's concerned scrutiny.

'I'm sorry if I've seemed to intrude in your affairs. Forgive me.'

'Oh, Jim, I'm the one who should apologize. I'm reacting like an adolescent. Have a nice weekend.'

'You too.' He gave her a smile, rose and walked out.

Ginger lay her head on her folded arms and tried to understand why she felt this mixture of anger and frustration. Why was everyone but her convinced she should fall in love with Cameron?

The word love lingered in her mind. A long time ago she had heard a definition of love as being 'a satisfactory sense of someone.' That unusual definition had remained somewhere in the back of her mind ever since. It also made sense. Did she feel that way about Neil, satisfied with him?

Her thoughts turned to his body. Satisfactory? There was no doubt at all that she desired him physically, had from their first encounter. What else? Was she satisfied with his intelligence? That was evident in everything he said and did. What about his emotional qualities? He had proved to be considerate of her, showed loyalty toward his friends, his marriage had broken up through no fault of his own, apparently. His aunts, although somewhat eccentric, obviously came from good stock, and he must have inherited some of those same sterling qualities. What was there not to like about the man?

'Only Colin,' she said in a whisper. And even Colin seemed to become more of a memory and less a part of her life with every passing day.

She sighed and raised her head again, surprised to find that her eyes were moist. Was she *that* intent on solving this riddle?

The telephone rang. She had not heard Neil's voice for several days, and the rich, deep timbre of it set her heart fluttering like the wings of a hummingbird.

'Ginger, I hope you don't have plans for the holiday.'

Of course she had none. Until he came along, her social life had been practically nonexistent. Every holiday, not merely the Fourth of July, became her Independence Day. Independence, in this case, meaning lonely.

'Actually — ' She spoke slowly, not wanting to sound too eager.

'Good,' he continued, taking her answer for granted. 'I'm told there's a small town on the peninsula that holds a great festival every year, food, swimming, sailing, even a carnival.'

'I've heard of it.'

'It sounds like a lot of fun and we can participate in the sports or just watch. I'm told it's practically the windsurfing capital of the world. Do you know how to windsurf?'

'I did it once or twice a few years ago.'

'Great. Then you'll go with me?'

In truth, she had no resistance for anything he might propose. She didn't want to be alone on another holiday; she wanted to be with people. Jim Blake had a girlfriend now and all her women friends were married. Perhaps it wasn't wise to spend so much time with Neil, but what could happen during a day in the sun?

'All right. That does sound nice.' She made her voice deliberately noncommittal, not eager.

'I'll pick you up at eight tomorrow morning so we'll be in time for the breakfast. Bring a swimsuit and towel and something warm for watching fireworks later. I'll have a blanket for sitting on the grass. It's all settled.'

Ginger hung up the phone. So it was all settled? Of course she would go, but her qualms about their relationship were far from settled. Yet, was she only fooling herself? How could she deny that since he had come along, she had finally begun to have moments of pure joy, happiness, with someone other than Colin? Could love come into her life again as well?

* * *

Ginger had lunch with Mary and Carrie Dillon that afternoon. Their conversation always surprised her and she enjoyed their company, although she wondered occasionally why she had become so close to women who were old enough to be her grandmother. It had nothing to do with being related to Neil, either. On that point she felt quite sure. She had come to love them for themselves alone. And their unique personalities.

She spent the first half hour trying to get them to buy back the shares of First Continental they had borrowed for their short sale. Short selling could be a risky business, and to think that these dear old ladies were involved bothered her more than she cared to admit. But they were adamant.

'But, look, my dear,' Mary said, protesting, 'the stock has gone down. Surely that means — '

' — we were right to sell,' Carrie finished. 'And it's not over yet. It's going to — '

'Go down some more,' said Mary.

'It's defying gravity,' Ginger said gently. 'The rest of the market seems to be going up. Look at the Dow Jones Industrial Average — '

'Our book says that stocks sometimes make cycles that don't coincide — '

' — with the market as a whole. And this is one of them. You mustn't be concerned. We know — '

' — what we're doing. Sometimes you sound just like our nephew. He thinks — '

' — we don't know what we're doing either, just because we're a little older. But we've been investing since — '

' — before he was born!'

Ginger enjoyed hearing them talk about Neil, especially since she hadn't initiated the conversation. It was like eavesdropping, but she didn't care. She only regretted that they hadn't been closer to their nephew, so she could learn even more about him.

'You didn't live near him while he grew up, though,' she prompted.

'No, we had moved out West by that time. Boston is too tame,' Carrie answered.

'But we kept in touch,' Mary added. 'We always knew what he did. There weren't a lot of children in our family, but — '

' — we were very close, nonetheless. We always sent him a gift on his birthday — it's the same day as ours, you know, and at Christmas and — '

' — unlike many children, he would write thank you letters and tell us all about his activities. We went to his graduation.'

'We helped him get his first job.'

Ginger lifted an eyebrow in surprise. Neil didn't seem the type to need help in anything. 'How did that happen?'

'Through a friend of Father's. He needed bright young people to train in his profession, and Neil accepted, but — '

' — just for a little while. Darlene made him give it up when he went to New York with her.'

'She's an actress and needed to be where the jobs were,' Ginger offered.

'Oh, I don't mean that part. She never liked him working for Father's friend.'

'What kind of work did he do? Who did he work for?'

'Pinkerton.'

'Pinkerton? The detective agency Pinkerton?'

'That's the one! Neil was a detective!' She beamed, as if she wished he were still a detective, or better yet, as if she wished she were one.

12

On July Fourth, Ginger and Neil drove down the Peninsula in his new red Porsche. After the revelation made by his aunts, her first impulse had been to cancel the excursion. The knowledge that he'd been a detective struck her like a blow to the midriff. Why hadn't he told her about it? She'd been right all along: there was something mysterious about him.

But another day of consideration changed her mind. She would go with him as planned. Free from the merciless ringing of her telephone and given privacy never found in her office — as well as neutral ground not afforded by her apartment — she could question him about this new discovery.

As each suspicion emerged, she countered it with the need to give him the benefit of the doubt. Her heart would not let her judge him too hastily, without a fair trial, as it were. If her leaning toward exonerating Neil meant she had begun to care deeply for him, then so be it. She would worry about the consequences of that later.

While she pondered these questions, Neil broke the silence. 'A penny for your thoughts,' he said.

'I was thinking in much higher terms, millions of dollars.'

He laughed gently before answering. 'I know about inflation but I didn't realize thoughts had escalated that much.'

'When we went to Sausalito a few weeks ago, you asked me about my attitude toward money. Now it's my turn to ask you about yours. What would you do, or not do, for money?' The question hung in the air for a moment and she thought she could hear the blood surge through her veins.

'Actually, like you, I don't take money very seriously at all.' He spoke in a quick, offhand manner.

'That's probably because you've always had it.'

'Not so.' His tone at once became solemn, and, as he looked steadfastly into her face, his eyes took on a darker shade. 'My aunts always had a bit of money and — heaven only knows how — they parlayed it into a considerable nest-egg. But my side of the family belonged to the great middle class. I had to work my way through college, and it was never easy.'

'And after that you traveled around Europe — '

'Bummed my way around Europe would be more accurate.'

' — staying in youth hostels.'

'Yes. Then I married Darlene and we went to New York.'

'Hold on a minute. Aren't you leaving out a few years?' She studied his profile while he kept his eyes on the highway.

'You didn't say you wanted a play-by-play account, and, frankly a lot of it was rather dull.'

'Not to me.'

He turned his eyes to her momentarily to give her a look that said he liked her wanting to know more about him.

'When you came back from Europe you didn't go to New York at once. How did you live? What job did you have?' She hated herself for this roundabout method of questioning.

'Oh.' He paused.

Would he tell the truth? Ginger's heart made a staccato beat while she waited.

'I worked for a detective agency.'

She felt her breath escape and realized she'd been holding it in. She turned her head to glance at the passing scenery for a moment, regaining her calm before continuing. His admittance brought sweet relief, yet she continued probing. 'But you didn't pursue that career in New York.'

'No. I'd always had an interest in writing and since I found myself in the publishing capital of the country, I

191

pounded on some publishers' doors. That didn't work, but someone suggested the *Wall Street Journal* and I got a very lowly job there. And then the stock market bug bit me, and here I am.' Once more his tone indicated he considered the subject closed.

'Were you good at it, the detective business, I mean?'

'I suppose so. It's not as glamorous a profession as movies lead us to believe. But then writing is not so glamorous either. Why do you ask?'

'I'm wondering why you didn't stay with it in New York.'

'It would have meant transferring to another office, not that that would have been so difficult, I suppose. I just didn't have sufficient interest.'

'So, you didn't ever work as a detective again?'

A frown creased his forehead. 'You apparently want to know something else and I'm not giving you the right answers. Why don't you just ask me point blank?'

Ginger swallowed first. 'You're not a detective now.'

'No.' Another pause. 'Are you concerned I might be? Is being a detective such a terrible thing in your opinion?'

'Not as long as you don't investigate me.' The words tumbled out before she could realize how they might sound.

But he laughed. 'Of course not.' Then he flashed a look of complete admiration over her. 'Ginger, I don't need a reason to want to be with you. You are far too attractive for that.'

She supposed that did explain things. Why did she constantly feel she needed to know more? He turned the car off the freeway as they neared their destination. Further questioning, if she felt the necessity, could wait for later in the day. For the moment the bright sun warmed her skin and the fresh air smelled of popcorn and cotton candy. As they approached the site of the carnival, the crowds of people and the colorful tents and umbrellas claimed her attention. Her mood changed from brooding over his past to enjoying his present company.

After their pancake breakfast, served on long tables on a grassy knoll, they strolled behind the recreation center building and saw that dozens of sailboards dotted the surface of the lake.

The bright dacron sails, as well as the colorful clothing of everyone on the boardwalk and grassy bank, made a kaleidoscope of greens, reds, blues, yellows. Ginger and Neil, wearing swimsuits underneath, stripped off their pants and shirts and found the young man who rented sailboards. Ginger chose one outfitted with a patriotically red, white and blue sail, to match the swimsuit she had chosen for the day, while Neil picked one with black and yellow stripes against a white background.

It took Ginger several tries and a few tumbles into the water before she regained the knack. Neil, on the other hand, took off immediately and went skimming across the water. When she had again mastered the technique of keeping her balance, at the same time letting the wind fill the sail, they took off together and raced downwind. Exhilarated, Ginger thrilled to their darting over the blue-green water and occasionally passing other sailboards. Half an hour later, the constant motion had finally tired her. She seemed to have a life-or-death hold on the bar, her toes gripped the board, and the taut muscles of her legs throbbed.

'Let's go back,' she shouted to him.

He nodded, and, watching out for other sailboards through the clear plastic insert in the sail, Ginger maneuvered back up the lagoon, stepping around the sail each time she tacked. She lost sight of Neil at one point and expected he had gone ahead of her and would be waiting at the dock where they'd started, but when she swirled in, he was nowhere in sight. Moments later he joined her, just in time to see her misjudge the wind in the cove, luff her sail and fall into the water.

When she came to the surface, curls dripping, Neil reached down to help her to the boardwalk. 'Where were you?' she asked. 'I thought you'd beaten me.'

'Oh, were we having a race? I stayed behind you all the time, making sure you were okay.'

'As you see,' she said, laughing at herself. His concern touched her and a deep longing welled up inside her again. How could she not respond to his constant gentle consideration? Like many modern women, she knew she could take care of herself, but too often messages of caring and concern were forgotten. She was not too modern to appreciate warm-hearted gestures.

'You did so well. How did you manage to fall down here?'

'Just lucky I guess.' She watched him return both boards to the row of rentals.

'Let's sit on the grass and relax.' Neil

started to take her hand to lead the way, but Ginger shook her hair, sending a spray of water all over his tanned body, and he backed away, toward the water's edge.

'You have to remember,' she said, still breathing heavily, 'I've had far more exercise than you this morning. You haven't even had to swim a stroke!' With her last sentence, she put her hands on his broad chest and pushed him playfully. Off-balance, he slipped on the wet boards and hurtled into the water, then came up sputtering to the sounds of her laughter.

'Gotcha!' she said, pointing a finger at him.

'I surrender,' he answered, slapping the water and sending sprays upward. 'Is this enough exercise for you?' He lowered his head and swam for several yards, then returned and, the muscles of his upper arms taut and shiny, hauled himself up onto the dock in one smooth, graceful movement.

They walked up the grassy hill

toward where they had left their clothes and towels. Neil pulled a small green and red plaid blanket out of his tote bag and spread it under a nearby tree. 'Sit here, I think you've had enough sun for awhile.'

Grateful again for his thoughtfulness, Ginger felt guilty. 'I'm sorry I pushed you. That was childish of me.'

'I enjoyed the swim. And anyway — ' his voice dropped, low and cool ' — I'll get even with you later.'

'What do you mean by that?'

'Nothing. Just — ' He stopped, apparently unwilling to reveal his thoughts.

Would he try to make love to her again? Would she let him? She dried off and sat down, letting her gaze sweep over the scene below them, barely conscious of the colorful sails and sparkling water, stark white buildings with yellow awnings and blue tiled roofs that nestled on a small island, and, beyond them, the bay and the eastern hills.

A comfortable silence settled over them, as each engaged in private thoughts. Ginger's were of Neil, of how he was slowly pushing Colin from her thoughts. And perhaps that was just as well. She couldn't continue to live in the past. Finally she realized he had been staring at her for some minutes. Her own thoughts, as well as what she imagined he was thinking, made her nervous. It would never do to be so serious so early in the day. She broke the mood.

'What are you looking at? Are my ears on straight? I did dress hurriedly this morning,' she joked.

His grin flashed briefly and then turned into a forced frown. 'As a matter of fact, there is something wrong with this ear.' He bent close and suddenly she felt his tongue swirl around the curves and slip inside. A delicious surge swept through her body. Prickles rose on the flesh of her arms. She tilted her head away from his mouth and looked into his eyes, twinkling with mischief.

Or something more?

'Don't you believe in privacy for ears?' Her aroused sensations were far from being as light-hearted as her words.

'If I can see it, I want to touch it,' he murmured. 'And that goes for every inch of you.'

She felt the warmth rising on her skin, thinking of the erotic areas he might touch that were not covered by her skimpy one-piece swimsuit.

'Could I touch you here?' he asked, and his forefinger traced a path along the edge of her suit where the fashionable cut had raised it high on her hip. 'Or here?' and the finger drew a line all the way down her back. 'Or here?' Leaving one hand at her back, he brought the other up and outlined the top edge of the suit, toward the swell of her breasts.

Still, Ginger didn't move. She thought, not of being in public with him, but in her apartment: the way he looked at her and her sudden longing to have his hands caress her. She almost wished she had let him lick the wine that had spilled, his tongue gliding over her body, tasting her flesh.

All at once his hand pressed more firmly on her hip. She probed his deep brown eyes with hers, saw blatant desire written there. Yes, her body told her.

But she knew it lied. Yes, you wouldn't run from him now, would you? But that's because it's safe. You know nothing will happen in front of a thousand people. So your body responds and you pretend you'll let him make love to you.

Disturbed by the ambivalence of her feelings, she moved under his touch. At once his hands dropped away and one rested on the blanket between them. The other pushed his hair back from his forehead in a gesture that told Ginger he had been deeply affected by the intimacy of the moment.

She rolled off the blanket and lay in the grass, feeling the prickly spears give way beneath her. The sun shone high, brilliant in a blue canopy of sky that contained not a single cloud. She closed her eyes against its brilliance.

Neil lay down close to her, and soon his lips brushed hers in a feathery, light kiss.

Her eyes flew open, and she raised up on one elbow. His body loomed very large next to hers, his broad chest, long arms and legs, sturdy and muscular. The skin was bronze, but as she looked closer, she saw the color was uneven.

'I know how you get so tan,' she said. 'Your freckles just all run together!'

He laughed and rolled over onto his back. 'My secret is out. Now you won't love me anymore, having learned I am not suntanned at all, but merely one king-size freckle!'

She punched his arm playfully. 'You're the largest freckle I've ever seen!' The word 'love' had not escaped her notice, but she refused to comment on it. She wanted only light-hearted bantering that day.

She jumped up. 'My suit's dry now; I

think I'll change back into my clothes and we can look over the exhibits.'

'Sure, if you like.' He rolled the blanket and stuffed it into his black nylon bag. 'Meet you back here in ten minutes.'

Almost fifteen minutes had gone by before Ginger had dried herself thoroughly, put sunscreen on her bare skin and slipped into her pants and blouse again. Then she added a touch of color to her lips and raked a comb through her disheveled hair. When she emerged from the wooden dressing room kiosk, she saw Neil standing some distance away, talking to another man.

She hesitated, not knowing whether to approach or not, for the man was a stranger, dressed not like everyone else in the park, in a bathing suit, or sports clothes, but a suit and tie. His eyes were shielded by large, mirrored sunglasses.

Neil appeared just as odd. He had already changed back into his slacks and shirt, but he held his tote bag tightly under one arm, his other hand apparently inside the bag. From her position, she couldn't see Neil's face, but that of the other man seemed intense, as if he were arguing, or else giving information at a very fast clip. Just as she decided to join them, the other man, shorter by several inches than Neil, began to back away, but Neil stepped even closer to him. Why? What was going on?

13

Ginger felt strongly that something mysterious was underway, but she moved forward. 'Hi,' she called.

Neil spun around. 'This gentleman wants to know the way to Gull Avenue but, being a stranger here myself, I haven't been able to help him, unless you know.'

The thought of them discussing directions had never entered her mind. 'No.'

The stranger nodded, walked rapidly up the crest of the hill and jumped into a black car double-parked at the curb. Ginger let Neil take her arm and propel her toward the recreation center, but nagging thoughts disturbed her. Why didn't the man ask someone else for the information he wanted? Another mystery added itself to all the others about Neil Cameron. Every time he explained one, another seemed to take its place.

But what could she say? Probably only her vivid imagination turned the stranger's casual question into something sinister. Most likely of all, her fear of falling in love with Neil threw obstacles in her path.

Strolling through the booths of artists and craftspeople surrounding the recreation center building, Neil kept one hand lightly under Ginger's elbow, guiding her through the crowds. As usual it made her feel comfortable, safe.

Besides oil paintings, watercolors and photographs, there were wood-framed mirrors for sale, children's clothing of yarn or appliqued fabric, stained glass hangings and windows, hand-crafted jewelry, pottery, and painted weather vanes carved into the shape of ducks.

Neil steered her to one particular booth and purchased a long hand-painted silk scarf, which he draped around Ginger's neck and tied in a rakish bow at the side. 'There,' he announced, 'If I were a knight in a joust, you would now be my lady.'

He moved off, then looked back to see her standing still.

Did she want to be his 'lady'? Would she ever know? Not if these strange things kept happening. 'It's not as easy as that.'

'No harm in trying.' He gestured with one hand, returned to her side and tilted her chin to him. 'I do want you to be my lady, you know.' The words were hushed, a mere whisper that no one else could hear. She felt her heart respond to him, but she could think of nothing appropriate, not while her emotions were so ambiguous.

Next they tried the contest booths, hurtling baseballs at bottles that refused to fall down, and pennies into jars that apparently had no openings after all. The games supported various philanthropic groups whose names were boldly, if unprofessionally, painted on overhead signs, and they giggled and shouted with the many other people doing the same thing. When finally Neil won a small stuffed bear for her, they were as joyful as if they'd won a cruise to Hawaii.

Clutching her treasure, Ginger chose a spot under a tree while Neil headed for the food displays to buy fried chicken, corn on the cob and garlic French bread for their dinner. She spread the blanket neatly on the grass, then realized that in pulling it from the tote bag, something else had tumbled out, a small tape recorder. The turbulence in her middle returned. Why would he bring a tape recorder to this outing? Before she could give the riddle more consideration, he returned and, as if she were somehow guilty, she pushed it back into the bag.

'After we eat, we'll find a good location to view the fireworks.'

Ginger put her questions aside temporarily, but later, as they waited at the crest of the hill for the display to begin, she decided to reopen the subject. 'So you worked for a detective agency?'

'Very dull stuff.'

'But I want to know about it.'

Ginger said the words quickly, then realized her motives were painfully obvious. But then, would she be here with him now if she didn't want to know all about him? He would have to be extremely obtuse — which was emphatically not the case — not to suspect a deep interest in him lay behind the probing.

'We went to New York and I got a job writing.' He closed his eyes, as if he could see the past more clearly that way, before resuming. 'As I said, we didn't have much money. Darlene pounded on agents' doors, getting occasional work as a model, and my job barely paid the rent, with not much left over. But I spent a lot of my free time in a brokerage office watching the tape; you know, like the people do in your own office.'

'The ones in our office all look like retired gentlemen who have nothing better to do. Except during the lunch hour, of course,' she added.

'Well, I became one of those. It fascinated me. And, since I worked there, I read the *Wall Street Journal* from cover to cover every day. Finally I began to invest some money.'

'But if you were poor, how did you do that?'

'My aunts had just sent me a rather large check for my birthday. You see, by coincidence, our birthdays are the same, so they've always remembered me.'

'And you they?'

'Naturally. Although in those days, all I could afford to send them in return was a studio card with some outrageous message on it.'

'What kind of message?'

'Like, 'Don't worry if your birthday cake is loaded with preservatives. At your age you need all the help you can get!''

Ginger's laugh erupted and the people nearby turned their heads in her direction. She dropped her voice. 'They liked it?'

'Loved it. They're the greatest aunts in the world. Everyone should have a set.'

'So a crazy sense of humor runs in the family.'

'At any rate, instead of something practical, I used their check to buy shares of a stock I'd been following and the thing took off about three months later and made me a lot of money.'

'Really?'

'Well, not filthy rich, but enough so I knew that's what I wanted to do from then on. It looked so easy.'

'You're not going to tell me everything you picked from then on made money?'

'Of course not. I had frequent losers, just the same as everyone else. But I developed a market timing theory.'

'Just like — ' She'd been about to comment that his aunts were into a market timing theory before she remembered she had been warned not to speak of their investments. 'Timing?'

Neil paused and a tiny frown flitted

across his forehead before he resumed. 'Sort of. Anyway, it seemed to work pretty well, and I quit the newspaper to invest full time.'

'Your success must have made things easier for Darlene.'

'The marriage had broken up by then.' He said the words in a tight, clipped fashion.

'Oh, I'm sorry.'

He sighed. 'She left me long before my theories began to pay off. She accused me of being afraid of hard work, of getting my hands dirty in a real job.'

'That's a strange accusation.'

'Acting is very hard work, you see. She pounded the pavements day after day, trying, always trying. And she took acting lessons, singing lessons, dancing lessons, anything that might help her break in. It was exhausting. I admit it.'

'That was no reason to berate you for what you were doing.'

'Perhaps not, but I could understand

her point. I *should* have been more aware of her needs and feelings.' He paused, as if remembering his part in the marriage's failure. 'She got a small part in an off-Broadway play finally, and, frankly, I think one of the men in the cast had a bit to do with the breakup. I suspected they were having an affair.'

Ginger felt a pounding in her chest, almost as if the pain he must have suffered then transferred itself to her. In a soft voice she asked, 'What did you do about it?'

'Nothing. I had apologized for my inadequacies as a husband, tried to make it up to her, hoped the affair would blow over when the run of the play ended.'

'And did it?'

'I don't know. She moved out.' His voice was barely audible.

'Did you get the divorce then?'

'Neither of us could afford it at that time. Then later, when I started making money, I kept hoping she might return.

I always kept in touch with her, went to her plays. She got more and better parts during the next five years.'

'But she didn't come back,' Ginger filled in. Had Darlene done so, Ginger would not be with him today. Yet she sympathized with his agony.

'Actually she did.' Again Neil paused. He lifted one arm and rested it across his forehead, as if the gesture could hide the painful past.

'I had moved to a better apartment than the one we'd shared, and one night she turned up, bags in hand. I was so happy I almost cried. She stayed about a week.'

'I don't understand.'

'It turned out I had done well enough to suit her purposes. She wanted me to give her money so she could support her current boyfriend, who hadn't as much luck as she, but too much pride to live on her income. He apparently hadn't too much to live on mine!' His voice had not risen in volume but acquired a bitter edge. 'And she didn't mind sleeping with me in order to get it!'

Ginger was silent, unable to think of what to say that would comfort him. She almost regretted starting him on that road into the past, causing him to relive it. She stared down at him and wished she could cradle him in her arms, kiss away imaginary tears, comfort him.

Suddenly he shook his head as if to clear it, and sat up straight. 'God, whatever made me say all that?' His mood changed abruptly. 'I'm sorry, Ginger. That happened a very long time ago, and I'm quite over it. She got the divorce and some money and now she's doing very well. I'm happy for her but I have no regrets. No one's immune from making mistakes, and that marriage had been a mistake for both of us.'

The sky had darkened, deep blue rose in the east and golden red and yellow followed the sun as it sank westward. Street lights across from the park came on, resembling a line of soldiers carrying torches, marching down the street and along the bridges over the winding lagoon. She looked at them instead of into Neil's face, pulled her sweater from her bag and settled it around her shoulders, not answering. He put his hand over hers as soon as she returned it to the blanket and patted it, as if to say he expected no reply. The fact that he seemed to want to comfort her after his confession instead of seeking consolation from her, brought sudden tears to her eyes. Her earlier doubts dissolved into tenderness.

The fireworks began with several small bursts and then increased in size and intensity until they climaxed half an hour later with loud booms and at least a dozen huge displays, colored mostly in reds, whites and blues.

People surged toward their cars, and straggling children lit sparklers, giggling in the darkness.

Ginger picked up her things and followed Neil back to the parking lot, no more disquieting thoughts surfacing to mingle with memories of the pleasant day. They were a long time leaving the little town, its one road clogged with traffic, but finally they arrived at Ginger's apartment again and Neil took her in his arms in her living room.

He took the stuffed bear from her hands and dropped it into the wing chair, pulled her body close to his, stared into her eyes as if willing her to respond to his desires. At first his lips teased, brushing hers lightly, then his tongue probed the soft interior of her mouth, joining with hers.

She felt as if the fireworks they had seen erupted again, this time in the middle of her body, shooting sparks melting her insides. Her sudden need for him made spasms along her spine, and when he groaned her name against her mouth, his every pulse beat seemed to be part of her, pounding in her ears like cannon.

His arms completely circled her

waist, so that she felt his fingers along her ribs, slipping under her blouse, leaving burning places on her midriff. Hunger for him swept over her like molten lava, and she willed him to pick her up in those strong arms, carry her to her bed and —

The vision of her bed rose in her mind, even as his kisses rained on her cheeks and eyelids. Her bed, that she had shared with Colin. Her body tensed and instantly Neil let her go. He had sensed her withdrawal. The man was clairvoyant!

His speech was slow, soft, hoarse. 'The time will come, Ginger; I know it will. You are my lady.' The scarf he had purchased for her still lay loose around her neck, and he pulled it free and placed it instead around the neck of the little stuffed bear. 'You keep it,' he addressed the toy animal. 'Give it back to her when she's ready.'

Then he turned to Ginger again. 'It's not a leash, Ginger. It's not to tie you to me so that you have no freedom. It's only a symbol of a love that might link us together. That no matter what we do or where we go, there's an invisible bond between us that can't be broken.'

After another brief kiss on the top of her head, he turned and left the apartment. The bear smiled foolishly at her, but Ginger did not feel foolish when she kissed it on the tip of its shiny black nose.

14

Ginger picked up her telephone and rang the Dillon sisters. Since the last time she'd seen them, she'd spent an entire day with their nephew, and although she would have loved to discuss him with his aunts, that was not the purpose of her call.

'This is Mary Dillon.'

'It's about your short sale.' The papers in the open file on her desk seemed somehow accusing. 'I wondered if you were ready to close out your position. The stock has dropped over ten points — ' She glanced over at the numbers on the computer screen. ' — twenty-nine and a half now,' she continued, 'and with the averages continuing to make new highs, I just think — '

'Thank you for your concern, my dear, but we want to hold our position.'

'Are you quite sure? You didn't tell me your objective at the time you made the transaction, but I would think that a thirty per cent drop would be more than adequate — '

'It's really not time yet. But thank you again.'

'Miss Dillon,' Ginger said more loudly, fearing the lady would break the connection any moment, 'a drop like this in a stock that otherwise seems strong can spell some sort of trouble. Something may not be quite right in that company.'

'Oh dear, have you heard anything we ought to know?'

'Actually, no — ' Guilt that perhaps she had not investigated the company as thoroughly as she might warmed her face and stilled her tongue.

'Then we'll stay the way we are. By the way, we'll call you soon for another luncheon meeting. We can discuss it then if you like. So much nicer than on the telephone, don't you think?'

'Miss Dillon, I know I have nothing

concrete, but my feelings are strong that you should — ' Ginger had not heard the click on the other end of the line, but became suddenly aware of a dead sound. Finally the dial tone hummed.

'What have you been buying for my aunts?'

Ginger whirled around in her chair so quickly she felt her nylons snag on the corner of the desk. 'Neil!'

Coatless, his broad shoulders taut against the silky fabric of a pale blue shirt open at the throat, Neil came into the room, but did not sit. Instead he stood over Ginger, a frown creasing his forehead. 'What's going on?' he repeated.

'Nothing's going on.' Ginger looked down at her desk, instead of into his intense stare. When had he come in? How much of the conversation had he heard? She had been sworn to secrecy by his aunts, but if he heard her last few sentences, he must be aware that she had attempted to give good advice.

'I don't mind losing money myself,' he said, 'but I hope you're not playing games with the capital of two elderly women.'

'Playing games?' Ginger's own defenses soared and she stood up, making herself as tall as possible. 'I don't 'play games' with anyone, especially not with your aunts!'

'Then what were the strong feelings you mentioned?'

Ginger opened her mouth to tell him, but quickly closed it again. His tone of voice intimidated her. She felt wounded. Where was the sweet and tender man of yesterday? That man would not force her to betray his own aunts. She swallowed hard and dropped her voice. 'I'm not at liberty to say anything about the transactions of my clients.'

'That sounds like a cliché.' He sat down and suddenly his demeanor changed and his voice softened. 'I'm sorry if I sounded belligerent just now. But I would like to know what stock

223

you've purchased for them and why there's apparently some danger in it.'

Ginger was glad he'd returned to the charming, considerate man she was beginning to fall in love with. Still, she couldn't give in to his request. His aunts had made it very clear, on more than one occasion, that their transactions were strictly confidential and not even their nephew was entitled to know about them. She sat down too and looked across the desk at him.

'You know I can't tell you that. It would betray the broker-client confidence.'

'I'd hope my natural concern for my aunts would outweigh any consideration of confidentiality. We're talking family here.'

'I know, but I just can't do that. Why don't you ask them yourself?'

For several seconds, he looked steadfastly and seriously into her eyes. Then, finally, the tiny frown that creased his forehead disappeared and he smiled. Her heart leapt. The tightness in her chest dissolved and she felt as if she were grinning from ear to ear.

He stretched across the desk and captured her hands in his. 'Would you have dinner with me tomorrow night?'

'Of course. Is that what you came to see me about? You could have phoned, you know.'

'What? And miss a chance to look at the most beautiful stock broker in San Francisco? Not on your life!' He touched her palm to his lips before dropping her hands and getting to his feet. 'I may be working late. Would you mind terribly meeting me at my office?'

'Not at all. In fact, I'd like to see your new office.'

'Great. See you at six o'clock then.'

Before she could agree, he was out the door and she put the hand he had kissed up to her own mouth, as if she could still feel the imprint of his lips on it.

She had to stop that. She was acting like a silly schoolgirl. How long ago it seemed since she had assured herself that they could be merely friends. Then every time they were together a little piece of her armor chipped away. She had let him caress her. No, encouraged it. She knew she could no longer resist him.

She picked up a pencil and began to doodle on her notepad. Not silly drawings, but words, a list of pros and cons about Neil. Pro: he was handsome, kind, generous, intelligent. Con. She stopped, unable to think of anything negative to write except the one major problem: the mysterious things that kept happening. He hadn't told her he was a detective with Pinkerton until she found out from his aunts, but then he admitted it and made it sound quite normal. But no sooner were her doubts about that erased than she discovered he'd brought a tape recorder to the picnic. And then there was the man who spoke to him in the park. What was that all about?

She should have asked Neil about that right away, but for some reason she felt it would be an imposition. If she needed to know about something, surely he would tell her.

*   *   *

Like a spectator at a steadily unfolding drama, she spent the rest of the day, and most of the next, watching the price of First Continental fall. She went about her work as if a mere automaton, while Neil and his aunts occupied her thoughts.

Then, at last, just minutes before the Exchange closed for the day on Friday, the telephone rang and Carrie Dillon called to say that they would close out their position in First Continental. She wanted Ginger to buy back the shares they had sold previously and cover their short. Ginger uttered a long, obvious sigh and executed the order faster than anything else she had ever done.

Feeling a burden had been lifted

from her shoulders, she felt almost lightheaded that afternoon. Taking her purse from the lowest left-hand drawer of her desk, she marched out of her office, signed out at the receptionist's desk and hailed a taxi.

Within minutes she arrived at Neil's office. The elevator whisked her to the fifth floor and she walked a short distance down the hall to number 508. She saw the name 'MacKenzie Neil Cameron' neatly lettered in gold on a black rectangle, turned the knob and entered.

He sat behind a broad modern desk of black and chrome, its top totally empty except for a closed portfolio and the telephone into which he spoke. He got to his feet the moment he saw her and beckoned her to come in, continuing his conversation in a tone that suggested he couldn't wait for it to end.

Ginger looked around the office. Two black leather chairs posed neatly in front of the desk, and, against the left-hand wall, another chair sat next to a potted plant. In the right corner a single file cabinet looked shiny, black and new. There were no papers, books or anything else in the room. She closed the door softly behind her, but did not enter further.

Within seconds, Neil hung up the phone, and came around the corner of his desk. 'Ginger, I'm so glad you're here.' He took her hands in both of his, and at once the pressure of his touch sent shivers through her arms.

'I like your office,' she said, pulling her hands free and walking past him to the window to look out at the traffic below.

'I didn't expect you to be early. If I'd known — '

'You'd have cleaned up the mess.'

He laughed. 'Listen, I ought to apologize.'

'What for?'

'I'm afraid I was a little short with you yesterday when I heard you on the phone with my aunts. I took your advice and spoke to them and they informed me in no uncertain terms to mind my own business, which I should have done without being asked.' He grinned sheepishly.

'The situation that existed that day — uh, no longer exists. Everything turned out fine.'

They looked across the desk at each other and again he moved toward her. 'I knew you wouldn't do anything to hurt them.'

She smiled. 'I was a little defensive myself that day. Perhaps it's my red hair.'

'I wouldn't change anything about you,' Neil said. By now he had come still closer and touched her shoulders. She could feel the heat of his body through her silk print dress. 'Especially not the red hair. I need someone just as fiery-tempered as I am to keep me under control.'

She knew she should move away from his touch, yet somehow her body refused to consider it. Instead, she leaned slightly toward him.

His arms slid down to her elbows, then to her back where he pressed her to him gently. Slowly his head bowed to hers and she lifted her face for his kiss. Its sweet, gentle, unpressured touch told her he put her under no obligation to him, but that he cared for her. A happy satisfaction spread through her body.

He broke the kiss, but, still holding her, he murmured, 'We'd better get out of here or they'll lock us in. How about that dinner?'

'Yes, I'm famished.'

'But first, I must make a phone call. Would you be an angel and go down to the garage and get my car? It would save some time.' He handed her a set of keys and a ticket stub. 'This will handle the fee. As an office-holder, I get free parking.'

'No, I don't mind. Where is it parked?'

'The lowest level, E, I believe it is.'

'All right.' She hesitated another moment, slipped the ticket into the side pocket of her dress.

He reached for her and planted a kiss on her forehead. 'I'll meet you outside in a few minutes.'

The slow elevator, as well as her search for his Porsche — which, because of its shape, was not easy to spot in the almost-full garage — took more time than she anticipated. Even so, she waited for him several minutes, parked in a 'no stopping' zone, and hoped a policeman wouldn't come by and insist she move. She was almost annoyed with Neil when he finally appeared. He opened the driver's door for her to slip out to the other side.

'Sorry to be so long, love.' But he grinned, obviously happy about something, and not, apparently, that sorry at all.

Still, the anticipation of spending several hours with him quickly erased her disappointment at having been kept waiting.

Neil eased the car from the curb and headed back toward the congested downtown streets of the city. 'I thought we'd have a drink at the Iron Horse first. Is that all right?' Before she could answer, he continued. 'They make a drink called a 'Brandana' that you might enjoy.'

But, once seated in the dimly-lit cocktail lounge with their concoctions of creme de banana, brandy and cream before them, Neil again excused himself to make a telephone call and stayed away for almost ten minutes. Anger and frustration welled up in Ginger's breast. What was going on now? Just when she felt so close to him, trusted him, he began his mysterious act all over again. Fears, like little mice, gnawed at her insides.

15

Wisps of grey fog curled over the towers of the Golden Gate Bridge as Ginger and Nell crossed it, driving north. After going through the tunnel, they saw more fog creeping down from the hills and threatening to engulf the highway.

'I love the city,' Neil said, taking his gaze from the winding road for a moment to glance at Ginger, 'but you have to admit the summer is not as warm here as people expect.'

'We're just naturally air conditioned, that's all. But by September and October, the fog doesn't move in from the ocean and chill the air. Even the nights are warm then.'

'I'll believe that when I see it, or, rather, feel it,' he answered. 'Actually there's a lot to be said for a place where you can sleep under a blanket every night of the year. I like being cool at night.'

Soon he turned the car off the highway and drove through winding streets that first went down, then up. The street became narrower as they ascended into a residential neighborhood, and the trees grew thicker, blotting out some of the light. At last he pulled into the driveway of a split-level redwood-sided house and announced, 'Here we are.'

'Where? I thought we were going to dinner. This doesn't look like a restaurant to me.'

'I call it Casa Cameron. I live here.' Neil walked around to her side of the car to help her to step out, but she had not moved from her seat.

'You? But I thought you were living in an old Victorian in the city.'

'I'm only renting that on a month-to-month basis. I'm buying this.'

Pleasure and disappointment mingled in her reaction. On the one hand, it was heartwarming to know that he was a resident of the bay area now and would not soon leave her world. Still, he had purchased the house alone, and, inexplicably, she felt a small pang of jealousy that he had done so without sharing the occasion with her.

But again her common sense overrode her emotions. Why would he ask her, after all? They were only friends, he was certainly free to do anything he liked without her knowledge or consent.

'You're very impetuous. Buying a house is a pretty serious investment, not usually done on the spur of the moment.'

'I know, but it's a habit I find hard to break. Actually, I'm not completely moved in yet. I only signed the papers day before yesterday. Escrow hasn't closed, but since the building could also be leased, I paid them two months' rent in advance and asked for immediate occupancy.'

Ginger stepped out onto the sidewalk and followed Neil to the front door. A wide overhang from the roof covered the entrance, sheltering double doors carved from thick redwood. Neil unlocked them and led Ginger inside.

There was no furniture in the entry or the spacious living room beyond, but Ginger noticed the walls were painted oyster white except for one paneled in dark wood and containing a stone fireplace. Beneath their feet, thick cream-colored carpeting hushed their steps.

Neil took Ginger's hand and led her across the room. 'Let's see the view before the fog gets any thicker.' He pulled open the heavy white drapes, revealing a large redwood deck and, beyond, a magnificent view of San Francisco Bay, the Bridge and Angel Island. He slid open the glass doors and they stepped out.

'This is fantastic,' Ginger said. 'I have friends who have great views of the bay, but this is — well, I'm speechless.'

Neil put his arm around her shoulders and they stood at the railing of the deck for several moments, drinking in the view and the fresh air that smelled of the sea and the climbing roses that grew close by.

'It's lovely. I don't wonder you've bought it. Let me see the rest of the house.' She turned and stepped back into the living room.

'Let's start over here,' he said. The way led to a dining room, also with a sliding door and view of the bay, but, unlike the living room, it contained some furniture.

In the center of the room sat a small, low table of black lacquer, set with white plates, golden yellow napkins, shiny silver, and crystal goblets. Brass candlesticks held tall yellow candles and on each side of the table rested huge square pillows in the same golden yellow color, with black tassels at the corners. Ginger pulled her gaze from the sight and looked suspiciously at Neil.

'What's this all about?'

'Dinner, of course. I did promise

you.' He strode through an open doorway into a room beyond, still talking. 'And, if my guess is correct, dinner is ready.'

Ginger followed him into a modern kitchen and saw him reach for a large insulated hamper on the counter separating the working part of the kitchen from a cozy breakfast nook, again with a magnificent view of the bridge. He delved into the basket, pulling out covered containers that, judging by his handling of them, were piping hot.

'Just how did you manage to do all this?' she asked.

'The telephone is a marvelous instrument, did you know that?' He carried one of the dishes into the dining room, talking to her as he went. 'I'm afraid I had to neglect you a little this evening while I arranged things. You were marvelous about it, though.'

Ginger felt embarrassment creep up her face. She hadn't been marvelous about it at all. She'd been upset with him for his seeming rudeness, and only her eagerness to be with him, kept her from saying something about it. She was ashamed now of having doubted him. While she fumed, he'd been planning this surprise. How considerate. How thoughtful, and innovative.

'Let me help.' She reached for a dish and carried it gingerly back to the dining room, placing it in the center of the table. Three more trips put everything in place.

'Since the table is so low, you might be more comfortable if you slipped out of your shoes,' he suggested. He offered his arm and she rested hers on it, while she removed first one high-heeled pump and then the other. He led her to one of the cushions, then lit the candles.

Lifting the covers, he revealed Oriental food consisting of bowls of steaming rice, slivers of tender beef mixed with snow peas, celery, and onion in a savory brown sauce, chicken and almonds, huge prawns ready for dipping in sweet and sour sauce, even squares of pressed duck mixed with vegetables.

'I love Chinese food,' Ginger said, helping herself to a heaping spoonful of rice. 'How did you know?'

'I just hoped you'd like it. We have a lot in common, if you think about it.'

'Yes,' Ginger laughed. 'We both like to eat!'

He looked at her across the table, his eyes sweeping over her face, her throat, the square neckline of her dress and the single strand of pearls that rested on the silky fabric. 'Be serious.'

Ginger put a morsel of the pressed duck into her mouth and thought about the word. She understood her own feelings at last, but what were his? How serious was it for her to be in his house tonight? True, she hadn't known they were going to come there, but she could hardly be accused of resisting once she knew. Was it time to admit that mere friendship had nothing to do with the way she felt tonight?

The flickering light from the candles made shadows on his face, highlighting his nose, accenting his strong chin and cheekbones. His eyes had turned hazel again, with golden tints, as if they caught the light from the candles. A rush of emotion swept over her so that she could hardly swallow. She put down her fork and sipped some of the tea he had poured into tiny cups.

'All right,' she said, 'but remember you started this. Sometimes you do — mysterious things. I want you to explain them all to me. There, is that serious enough for you?'

He laughed before answering. 'Actually, I don't think I'm at all mysterious. I was a normal little boy, rode a bicycle at five, learned to swim at six, had a paper route, Boy Scout troop. I mean, we're talking All American kid here.'

'There you go again, always making jokes when I inquire about your past.'

'How much farther into my past do you want to go? Really, Ginger, there are no skeletons rattling in my closets. And turnabout's fair play. What subversive things were you into at the age of five?' After the barest pause, he suddenly said, 'What's your earliest memory of the Fourth of July?'

His words conjured up a vision of the most recent Fourth of July, the one spent with him. It had been her best, she thought. She forced herself to think back, to one many years before. 'I don't think it's the earliest, but the one that comes to mind is when I was about eight. My family planned to attend an amusement park with my cousin and her family, and after they arrived at our house, Betsy suddenly became ill and my father cancelled the excursion.'

'How disappointing for you. Couldn't some of you have gone anyway?'

'My aunt volunteered to stay home with Betsy, but I wouldn't go without her, so we all stayed home and I read stories to her. That evening, when she felt better, we went to see the fireworks and our fathers let us sit on the roof of the car to watch.'

'How sweet of you. And you an only

child. I always thought they were selfish little beasts.'

'No. Four of my best friends are only children.'

'So it turns out that single children are unselfish. I'm surprised.'

'Well,' Ginger admitted, remembering one person in particular with whom she had once had to work. 'Not all of them. But you see, we learn to share simply because we don't always have the opportunity to do it.'

'That doesn't make sense.'

'Yes, it does. When you have brothers and sisters at home, there's always someone to play with. But when you're alone, the times with playmates become precious, so you learn to be more considerate and polite with them, to find out what they want, to share, to please them.'

'Well, I suppose when you put it that way.'

'Look at your aunts,' Ginger added.

'What about my aunts?' His tone was slightly defensive.

'They're lovely ladies, I like them very much. But they have never married. They had each other, you see.'

'But they're certainly happy.'

'Oh, I'm sure they are. But my point is they were so happy with each other, they never had to make the effort to reach out to other people, to make friends, commitments.'

'Are you ready to make a commitment again, Ginger?'

The question came too suddenly: it caught her off guard. She'd been thinking of playmates, sisters, friends, not lovers or husbands to whom one committed oneself. 'Let's change the subject, shall we? Anyway, I think dinner is over.' Picking up her plate, she got to her feet.

While Neil poured more tea and pulled out a package of fortune cookies, Ginger carried the rest of the dishes into the kitchen. 'Shall we wash these?'

'Just put them back in the basket. The catering company will do it.'

'I must say I approve of that arrangement.'

He came behind her then, and put his arms around her waist, nestling his head in her hair. 'However, if you really want to get your hands wet, I can take care of that.' His voice caressed her, his breath warm on her neck.

'Yes?' Her own voice dropped almost to a whisper, and she smiled in anticipation of another of his surprises.

'There's a hot tub outside. Want to try it?'

She turned to face him, but he didn't allow her to escape the circle of his arms. 'It's late, it's dark, and the fog must be making it very cold.'

'The water won't be cold. I turned the heater on before dinner. Come on.'

They left the kitchen and, after picking up one of the dining room candles, proceeded through the house to the side yard. More sliding doors opened on another deck of redwood, this one with a single broad step leading to a small glass-walled garden. Surprisingly, it was neither cold nor foggy there, although they were outdoors with no roof overhead.

'Watch the step,' Neil said, and they eased their way toward a round hatch, which he lifted, revealing a deep redwood hot tub. Instantly swirls of steam rose, and Ginger could see water bubbling from jets on the inside edge.

'It looks very inviting, but I haven't a bathing suit.'

'Neither have I.' His tone was both droll and seductive.

Shivers swept over her arms and legs, and she visualized herself naked in the water with him. But she had no time to linger over the vision or do anything about it. She suddenly felt dizzy. Was it the steam rising from the tub or something she had eaten? No, it was the deck moving beneath her feet.

'That's odd,' Neil said. 'Look at the water. It's sloshing from side to side.'

Realization came and Ginger began

to laugh. 'Don't you know what's happening?'

'Is something happening?'

'You're in northern California. We're having a little earthquake.'

16

The 'little earthquake' went on and on. Neil took hold of Ginger's hand to steady her while everything seemed to tremble around them. Finally the shaking stopped.

'That was a big one,' she said, 'almost a minute, I think.'

'It seemed longer.'

'I know, they all do; but it only took fifteen seconds to topple a freeway a few years ago.'

'I remember reading about it. You don't suppose that's happened this time, do you?' He moved away and began to inspect the deck for signs of damage.

'That depends on the epicenter, although buildings can topple even thirty or forty miles away from the center.' Ginger followed him around the perimeter of the property, but saw nothing unusual.

'Look,' she said, pointing out across the Bay. 'The fog has lifted a little; I can see the lights of the city.'

He came close and put his arm lightly around her waist. 'It's still there, so I guess nothing much happened.'

They stood together silently for a moment and Ginger marveled again at the beauty of the city, the string of lights that paraded along the Bay Bridge, the glow of Coit Tower and the Transamerica Building. As usual, it enchanted her.

Finally they returned to the enclosed area and Neil stooped down to replace the redwood cover on the hot tub. 'Everything else seems to be okay, but the water isn't bubbling anymore, so apparently the power is out.'

'Sometimes, after an earthquake,' Ginger said, 'they turn off power deliberately in case lines are down. It keeps people from getting electrocuted if they happen to touch them.'

'Sounds sensible, but it ruins our evening.'

'It's time I was going anyway.'

He looked disappointed, but took her hand and led her through the garden to the side gate. 'We can get out this way. No need to go back in the house. He helped her into the Porsche, then pulled his car keys out of his pocket, got in beside her and started the engine.

As he negotiated the winding road, Neil drove down the hill slowly, the headlights of the car throwing swaths of light across the dense vegetation surrounding them. Then he slowed the car almost to a stop and Ginger saw people in the road ahead of them. What were they doing there at this time of night? Didn't they know it was dangerous to walk in the middle of a dark, winding road?

She leaned forward, peering out of the windshield. 'What's going on?'

'I don't know.' Neil inched the car forward until he came abreast of a man and woman hurrying forward. They turned their heads toward the Porsche and Neil rolled down his window to speak to them. 'What's the trouble?'

The man, fortyish, plump, wearing jeans and a heavy jacket, came closer. 'It was the earthquake,' he said. 'Trees fell over, power lines are down.'

'Where?'

The man pointed ahead. Ginger followed his gaze and then the headlights picked up still more people in the road.

Neil pulled the car off to the side as far as he could and, leaving the headlights on, stopped the engine. 'Let's have a look.'

Ginger scrambled out after him and they joined the others walking swiftly down the curving road. When they rounded the next bend, she saw what had caused the problem. Huge trees lay in their path, totally obliberating what lay beyond.

All around them, people were talking loudly, telling one another how the earthquake had felt to them, what had happened, and why they thought the trees were down.

'They were dead,' one man said. 'Should have been cleared out long ago.'

A woman picked up the story. 'The heavy rains we had this past spring must have washed out the hillside around them.'

'You got power?' someone asked another person.

'Nope. Lines are down all over.'

'What should we do?' Ginger asked Neil.

'I don't know. We sure can't drive down the hill with all that in the way.'

Ginger looked around, wondered where these people had come from. Where were their houses? Between the numerous trees surrounding them and no electricity to light them, they had disappeared as if by magic.

'Are the phones working?' Neil asked a tall man nearby.

'Yeah, someone's called 9-1-1 already. They know about it.'

Ginger shivered in the cold night air. She felt somewhat relieved that the authorities had been notified and soon help would arrive to clean up the mess caused by the earthquake. But what about right now? She looked at Neil expectantly.

He came close to her and spoke softly, reassuring. 'Nothing serious. We just can't drive back down the hill, that's all. They'll probably have it cleared by morning.'

Some of the people who had come to see what was going on were beginning to turn around and return to their homes. There was nothing to be done at the moment anyway.

'Is there any other way down? Can I get home tonight?' Ginger asked.

'Afraid not.' He paused. 'Look, at least we have a house to go to.' He led her back to the car, helped her inside, and then made a U-turn, heading back up the hill. 'It's not exactly the Mark Hopkins — actually it doesn't even have a bed — but we can at least stay out of the cold. I think we can manage just for one night.'

Ginger didn't answer. What could she say? Staying alone with him overnight hadn't been part of her plans, but there was nothing she could do about it. Was fate playing its little game with her, making it impossible for them *not* to make love tonight?

Back at his house, Neil opened the front door again and flipped the light switch, but nothing happened. 'I forgot, we're out of power. Good thing we have candles.'

As Ginger slowly followed him — at least there wasn't any furniture for her to bump into in the dark — he found the candles they'd used at dinner and lighted them. Then he pulled out the cushions they'd sat on and placed them in front of the living room fireplace. 'I never did light this,' he commented, 'but no time like the present. Lucky the previous owners didn't take these logs with them.'

Ginger sat on one of the cushions and watched him light some kindling underneath two logs in the grate. Then he sat on the other cushion and they stared at the flames.

After a long silence, he turned to her and put his hand over hers. 'Are you cold?'

'A little.'

He put his arm around her and pulled her close. 'You know,' he said, a slight tinge of laughter in his voice, 'I couldn't have done this better if I'd planned it.'

She didn't answer, knowing full well what he meant.

'Here we are alone together and you can't get away because of those trees in the road.' He raised one hand as if taking an oath. 'So help me, I did not arrange for an earthquake!'

She laughed.

Neil got up. 'I have a portable radio. We'll find a music station and dance to keep warm.' He took one of the candles and went into the dining room, then returned with a small radio. He placed it on the floor next to her, then took her hand and gently pulled her to her feet.

'May I have this dance?'

She stepped into his arms. 'Of course.' As they swayed to the music, his holding her close to him, his hand in hers, his arm around her back, she remembered a line from an old song: 'What is dancing but making love set to music?' She tried to break the mood that enveloped her. If *her* thoughts were becoming erotic, what about *his?*

'We can pretend we're not stuck here because of an earthquake,' he said. 'We're at the Ritz-Carlton, dancing to a fabulous orchestra and having a scintillating conversation.'

She was grateful for his light tone, as if he read her thoughts. 'I don't know if I can manage scintillating. What should we talk about?' She looked around. 'You have a lovely house. When did you plan to start living here?'

'Soon, I hope, but it obviously needs furniture and things. A woman's touch. Would you like to help me decorate it?'

'I'd be glad to try.' She paused. 'First you need a sofa. Something blue, perhaps. Do you like blue?'

'My favorite color.'

'And you'll need two lounge chairs, perhaps with blue stripes, and some tables. And Waterford crystal lamps. You can't depend on candles and the fireplace forever.'

'Waterford? You like spending my money.'

'Well you asked for my advice.'

'I wasn't complaining. You can decorate the entire house.'

'My, you're easy to please. Actually, you'll need to do a lot of shopping.'

'I'm afraid I'm not a person who could do that. You know, someone once told me the real difference between men and women. It's not that men are physically stronger, or that women have the babies. The real difference is that women like to shop.'

Ginger laughed. *'Touche'.'*

'Tomorrow you can go with me and choose everything I need to live here in comfort and style.'

'Everything? Are you telling me the

only furniture you have is that table? Or did the caterer provide that too?'

'No, it's really a coffee table and I bought it, along with a few other necessities, like a few towels and some kitchen utensils. There's a limit to how much a caterer will do, especially on short notice. I only requested a candelight dinner for two. I hope it met with your approval?'

'You know it did.' As he swirled her around in time to the music, she smiled up at him. 'So you're saying we won't go hungry, there might be food for breakfast?'

'If you like leftovers. Cold coffee.'

'Ugh.' She made a face.

'Well, without electricity we can't heat it up. But maybe the power will be back on by morning.'

'I hope so.'

The song ended and another started, a slow song that Ginger knew the words to, about love lost. She remembered hearing it soon after Colin was killed, and it always made her think of being in his arms. Now she was in someone else's arms, someone who thrilled her just as Colin once did.

As if he felt her mood, Neil's arms tightened around her and he pressed his cheek to hers. She closed her eyes and let herself feel the strength in his warm body against her own. Thinking of how they might have been together in the hot tub brought desire to the surface; she slid her arm down his back, holding him closer. He stopped dancing, turned his head and kissed her, at first softly, sweetly, then with growing passion. She responded, suddenly hungry for his kisses.

The radio announcer cut in abruptly with news of the earthquake. They broke apart and Ginger, weak-kneed, sank onto the cushion again and stared at the little radio, listening intently. The epicenter had been many miles north and only Marin County seemed to have been seriously affected. Trees and power lines were down in many places, homes damaged, but so far no reports of injuries or deaths.

'Thank goodness,' Ginger said aloud.

Neil didn't comment and they both listened to the announcer continue for several more minutes to report on the earthquake. Then, saying he'd be back with more news later, he ended his report and music played again. But Neil didn't get up and Ginger sat still too, staring into the fire.

'You're shivering,' he said. 'I didn't expect to sleep here for another week, so there's not much in the house, but I have a stadium robe in the trunk of the car. I'll get it.' Before he finished speaking, he was on his feet and heading for the door. Moments later he reappeared with a plaid wool lap robe which he wrapped around her.

She felt warmer, but doubts came to the surface. They were alone and, as usual, it had led to his kissing and caressing her. And now she was forced to spend the night with him. No going home. No sending him home. She wanted him — no doubt about that

— but now she felt helpless in the face of forces that seemed bent on forcing the issue. As if they were expected to take advantage of it, with no opportunity to choose if they should or not.

Again an awkward silence fell. 'Look,' Neil said at last, 'not only did I not bring on the earthquake, or knock down the trees, I never had any plans to seduce you tonight. Well, maybe only a tiny one.' He hurried on. 'If I'd meant to, I'd have provided a futon, at least.'

He paused and looked into her eyes again. 'I might as well admit it; if you'd been agreeable to going into the hot tub — '

'But I didn't bring a swimsuit — '

'I know. And afterward — '

'What made you think I'd be willing to do that?'

'I just hoped. You can't blame a guy for hoping.' He paused again. 'But the earthquake changed everything. We're stuck here and that means I can't try to make love to you. It's an unwritten law, you see: a gentleman doesn't take advantage of such a situation.'

Ginger smiled up at him. His little speech was endearing; but she couldn't help picturing them in the hot tub in his garden, darkness and steam surrounding them, warm water bubbling over them. *Stop!* she told herself.

'But we might as well try to get some sleep,' he added.

'Good idea.' She pulled the cushion into position as a pillow for her head. 'I feel guilty having the only blanket.'

'Don't. I'm very warm-blooded. I'll be fine. He lay down nearby, pushing his cushion into a pillow too.

Ginger tried to fall asleep, but her mind refused to settle down. She forced herself to stop thinking of Neil lying so close to her and instead thought of destroyed homes and property, those enormous trees blocking the road.

She was glad Neil didn't seem to need the robe, but the truth was she felt cold in spite of it. She raised her head slightly and saw that the fire had gone out: the two small logs had burned up some time ago.

She turned around to lie on her other side, pulling the robe tighter, trying to make a cocoon for herself. It was no use, she couldn't sleep.

Then she felt a movement and Neil tucked the blanket tighter around her and then hugged her to him, his chest against her back. 'I sensed you were cold,' he said. 'Just sharing some body heat. You can relax now. Go to sleep.'

Easy for him to say. Now that he'd promised not to make love to her, her traitorous body wanted precisely that. His warmth surged through the robe to her; the man was a living furnace. She sighed, at least she was comfortable; she wouldn't think about anything more.

17

Although they still had no electricity in the morning, at least the plumbing worked, and Ginger showered in luke-warm water, drying herself with one of the new towels Neil had purchased — no doubt for after using the hot tub — a few days earlier. However, she had to put on the same clothes she'd worn the evening before, including the silk dress and high-heeled pumps.

She found Neil in the kitchen. 'Cold Chinese food doesn't exactly appeal to me; why don't we find a restaurant for breakfast before I take you home.'

'You mean try to go back down the hill?'

''Try' is the operative word here,' he said. 'Frankly, I'm not optimistic about it. If they can't even get the power turned on yet, I don't see how they can have removed the trees.' He shrugged. 'But we'll have a shot at it.'

His pessimism was justified. The fallen trees still blocked the road. This time there were no people standing about, but something new had been added to the site. A large sign, hand-lettered in black, had been nailed to a stake in the ground next to the road. It read, 'Food and shelter at Church of Faith and Love. Two miles.' An arrow pointed back the way they'd come.

Neil turned the car around. After passing his own house, he drove further up the hill, found another sign. This one had nothing but an arrow and the initials 'CFL' and Neil turned onto the side road that dipped down before leveling out. Eventually they came to a parking lot with a few cars next to a large rustic building. A sign read, Church of Faith and Love. He pulled in and stopped. 'This must be the place.'

The main part of the building looked indeed like a church, with double doors in front, and a steeple. Attached to it on the right side, however, was another large building with a side door that stood open. They walked over to it, and, as they peered inside, a friendly voice greeted them.

'Come in. We have lots of food and hot coffee.'

The room was large, apparently a recreation room, and seemed to occupy most of the side building's space. Three smiling ladies, all in their fifties or sixties, stood behind a long table on which sat two large coffee urns, stacks of styrofoam cups, bowls of sugar, cartons of milk, plastic spoons, and four large platters containing homemade muffins, biscuits and fruit filled turn-overs. About a dozen people stood in front of the table, pouring their coffee or tea, helping themselves to the food, while others already sat on folding chairs at some of the round tables scattered throughout the room.

Two young women scurried between the tables and a doorway at the back of the room, which — judging by what Ginger could see through an opening cut into the wall — contained a fully equipped kitchen, where still more women were working.

Neil poured coffee for Ginger and spoke to the closest of the church ladies. 'I'm Neil Cameron,' he said, holding out his hand. 'I just bought a house down the hill a-ways. I didn't know there was a church up here.'

'Denise Warshow. Pleased to meet you.'

Ginger also shook hands with the woman. 'I'm Ginger Maddox. We don't have electricity at the house, but it would seem that you folks do.'

'We have a generator, thank goodness.' Ms. Warshow smiled again, looked confident, as if emergencies were no big deal. 'Help yourselves, folks.'

Ginger put a muffin and a turnover on a paper plate and took it, along with her coffee, to the table where Neil held out a chair for her.

As they ate, still more people began to arrive, and everyone seemed to be talking about the earthquake and its aftermath.

'Didja hear?' one man asked them. 'It's much worse farther north. Not just trees down, but houses, a bridge — '

'Not the Golden Gate Bridge?' Neil asked.

Another man laughed. He was tall and well-built with thick dark hair and a mustache. He looked about forty, Ginger thought. He had been walking through the room and now stopped to speak to them. 'No way is that bridge gonna come down. No, sir, nothing like that. Just a small one over a creek. Some roads collapsed too. Lots of people lost their homes.'

'That's awful,' Ginger said, feeling her pulse quicken. 'What will happen to them?'

'Some are gonna come here. We're turning this into a shelter tonight.' He paused, stretched out his hand. 'Name's Eric Warshow. My wife Denise and I are church custodians.'

Neil got up and shook hands with him and Ginger thanked them for the coffee and food. 'Have you heard when power will be restored, or the fallen trees removed?'

'Not yet. This is nothing compared to what's happened up north. Got to wait our turn. Meanwhile, if you folks can donate anything — We'll need more food, blankets, clothes, anything you can spare for the folks that lost their houses — '

'I wish we could,' Neil said, 'but as I explained to your wife a few minutes ago, I just bought a house here, and I haven't furnished it yet. We don't have a thing to donate. In fact, until we can get back to San Francisco, our only possessions are the clothes we're wearing, a couple of throw pillows and a radio.'

Eric Warshow laughed. 'Sounds like you need help.'

'I'd be glad to pay — ' Neil began.

Eric stopped him. 'No need for that.'

'Then can we at least *help* some-how?' Ginger asked. 'I'd be glad to do anything, help in any way you like.'

'You'll have to ask Denise, but I'm sure you can.' He rubbed a hand over his eyes, as if they burned from lack of sleep. 'Most of us have been up all night and could use a rest if someone else can take over.'

Neil volunteered too. 'I'm ready, willing and able to do my share.'

Eric looked him over. 'Not in those clothes. We'll get you some though. You, too, Ma'am.'

He went away and Ginger and Neil finished their breakfast. 'Are you sure you want to do this?' she asked him.

'Of course,' Neil answered. 'Everyone pitches in when there's work to be done. It wouldn't be the first time I dirtied my hands, you know.'

Ginger felt a wave of pleasure wash over her at his answer. Eric beckoned to him, and Neil got up and followed the other man. Denise Warshow provided Ginger with jeans and a tee shirt plus a pair of soiled tennis shoes. She found the ladies' room and changed into the donated clothing.

She remained in the kitchen all day. Just before noon, the staff changed, with the newcomers bringing boxes of food, and luncheon preparations began. Ginger made dozens of sandwiches — ham, turkey, egg salad — mixed up batches of lemonade, from time to time stirred the huge pot of soup on the industrial-sized stove. She ate her own lunch in less than twenty minutes sitting on a stool in a corner of the kitchen. Then she helped to clear it all away and began the preparations for a third meal.

At six o'clock Denise returned and told her to go into the other room to eat. 'Oh, by the way, P.G.& E. has the power back on again.'

'Does that mean the road is open?'

'No, not yet.'

Neil got up when he saw Ginger coming, and pulled out a chair. The jeans someone had given him were too short, but the plaid shirt, now dirt-stained, seemed made for a three hundred-pound man. Although he'd probably washed up before coming in, a black streak remained high on his forehead, and his hair needed a good brushing.

'Are you okay?' he asked.

'I'm fine. You?'

'Tired.'

They sat down in front of large plates of beef stew, bowls of cole slaw and thick crusty bread. Two other men sat at their table and they soon began to talk about what they'd been doing all day: searching through destroyed homes for what could be salvaged, shoring up only slightly-damaged buildings, removing debris, checking gas and water lines for leaks, and much more.

After eating their dinner, Ginger and Neil left each other again to do their separate chores. As it grew dark, some families began to arrive, including small children, clutching dolls or stuffed animals. Ginger felt a lump in her throat at the sight of them, and tears welled up in her eyes. She sprang forward to help them fill their dinner plates, then escorted them to cots where they could sleep, and handed out blankets.

Just before midnight Denise Warshow told Ginger that Eric was giving them two sleeping bags. 'You could sleep here if you want to,' she added, 'but if your house is okay you'd probably rather go back there.'

'Yes, I think so. Thank you very much.'

After helping Ginger into the Porsche, Neil got in next to her and drove back to his house. Once inside, he flipped the switch and the hall light went on.

'If we had those Waterford crystal lamps you're buying for me,' he said, 'we could do without the candles.' He retrieved the now much smaller candles, gave one to Ginger and headed for the hallway. He spread one sleeping bag in each of two bedrooms. 'Since we don't need the heat from the fireplace tonight, I thought you might like a little privacy.'

'Thank you. That's very considerate.'

Strange how awkward she suddenly felt with him. Something seemed changed about their relationship, but she didn't know what it was. She wanted to figure it out, but fatigue was closing down her mind. She felt as if she could sleep standing up.

'You worked so hard today, you must be exhausted, but if you need anything during the night just holler.' Then he was gone.

She fell into the sleeping bag without undressing. She missed Neil, wished they were snuggled close together as they'd been the night before. Wished — what? Her mind was still fuzzy. What was it that she needed to think of? Oh yes. She remembered now. She was in love.

★　★　★

On Sunday morning, Ginger awoke with the same feeling she'd had the night before; she loved this man. No one had ever affected her the way he did. No one seemed so unselfish and considerate, to say nothing of romantic. She felt more alive than she had in over a year. As they greeted each other in the kitchen she felt awkward and shy, wondered if her feelings were somehow etched on her face where he could read them.

He kissed her lightly, more like a friend than a lover, then stretched and groaned. 'Boy, am I out of shape! I ache in muscles I never knew I had!'

'Well, then,' she said, grinning, 'you'll be glad to know you get a chance to exercise them. Don't they call that 'hair of the dog' or something?'

'That's not 'hair of the dog,' but it'll do.'

When they arrived at the church, they were immediately put to work. The day was a repetition of Saturday. Ginger worked in the kitchen and recreation room, preparing food, serving food, hardly ever finding a moment to sit down and rest. Then, in the middle of the afternoon, when their parents had gone back to their damaged houses to see what could be salvaged, she supervised children.

Neil, too, worked as he had the day before, and that night they again left the church close to midnight and returned to his house. But this time he took her hand and led her outside to the redwood deck. He lifted the lid of the hot tub.

'I never turned this off the other night, so it's been bubbling away ever since the power went back on. What do you say we warm the kinks out of our bodies?'

She didn't answer and he hurried on. 'Underwear is okay, since we don't have swimsuits.'

Fatigue began to melt away and sleep lost some of its allure. Her muscles seemed to have minds and voices, urging her to soothe them in the

277

steaming water. 'All right.'

Neil went back inside and returned with the two candles and some towels. He turned off the outside light, leaving them in almost total darkness, until he put a match to the candles and two tiny flames lit the edge of the hot tub. Then he pulled off his pants and shirt and stepped into the tub wearing only briefs.

Ginger quickly stripped down to her panties and bra and slipped into the water too. The striking contrast between the cold air and the water made her gasp. But within moments after settling opposite Neil on the redwood bench that surrounded the inside of the tub, the temperature became bearable, and she felt utterly relaxed.

'We need to talk,' he said. 'I have some good news and some bad news.'

'What's the good news?'

'A crew has been working on removing those trees from the road; they told us it'll be open by morning.'

Ginger felt her pulse quicken. 'We

can get through?'

'I've already told Eric Warshow we won't be back. I can take you home tomorrow.'

'What's the bad news?'

'I can take you home tomorrow.' He paused. 'I don't want you to go.'

Ginger felt her face grow warm. She felt the same but didn't know how to tell him. 'We've had this whole weekend together.'

'Not together. You worked inside the church and I worked outside. We hardly exchanged two sentences.'

'We were helping people who needed us.'

'I know that, and I'm glad, but I have needs too, you know.'

What did he mean? Ginger turned her head away, sorting out her own needs. She wanted to spend her whole life with him.

'There's something else,' he said. 'I've known you a month — thirty-nine days to be exact — but it seems more like forever. I'm in love with you, Ginger.'

She felt her throat tighten and sudden tears sprang to her eyes. He loved her.

He stared at her without moving, as if waiting for her reply. But she couldn't speak. Visions of Neil whirled around in her head: watching the effortless way he did things, listening to his infectious laugh, feeling the warmth of his endearing smile, the passion of his kisses.

'Okay,' he said in a dejected tone. 'I guess you don't feel the same after all. I thought you knew I've loved you almost since the moment I first saw you. I thought — '

Finally she blurted out the words. 'I love you, too.'

He came to her and his arms went around her body, feathery light, like the steam that rose from the tub. Her fingers touched his bare skin, and desire began to build in her, like ocean waves coming in time after time from the ever-moving sea. His mouth closed on hers in a clinging kiss, and he pressed his naked chest against her body. She pulled her lips from his and kissed his cheeks and chin.

Candlelight threw his face into shadow. Was it the fog outside the glass enclosure or the steam from the tub that made everything hazy? His hands went to her back. Between moist kisses he unhooked her bra and removed it. She put both arms around his neck, while his hands slid over her body, finding every throbbing part of it, making her sigh with delight.

Again they kissed, the water swirling around her chin and dampening the hair at the back of her neck. A stream of water pulsed rhythmically at her side, and then it stopped, as Neil's arm came between her and the jet. While his strong smooth hands stroked her flesh, she slipped off her lacy briefs.

'Ginger, I want you to be mine always.' His voice was throaty and low and its huskiness excited her as much as the words themselves. The bubbling water swirled sensuously between them, and she moved against his body once more, felt the urgency of his aroused passion. Her breath quickened, her stomach muscles tightened, and her skin seemed to melt into his flesh.

She closed her eyes and rested her head against the edge of the tub, while the mist rolled over her face like cool fingers. His mouth came down on hers, soft but firm, his lips moist, warm, steamy. She held him close, feeling his long, hard legs next to her own, the hairs of his chest tickling. Pulsing, pounding sensations urged her forward and she pressed herself against him, on fire for still more of him.

He kissed the salty drops of perspiration on her upper lip, licked the beads of moisture that ran down her neck, and caressed her tenderly.

She felt her body react to his. She stroked the sides of his face, held him still closer to her burning flesh, while shudders raked her from within. 'Make love to me.'

He paused only a moment, then

stood up, grabbed one of the towels, and lifted her effortlessly out of the tub. He carried her, wrapped in the towel, back into the house. Pale light illuminated the interior just enough for him to negotiate the corridors and he entered the bedroom she'd slept in the night before and lay her gently on the sleeping bag.

He patted her body slowly with the towel, his movements bringing a heightened response; then he dried himself hurriedly. The sight of his naked body, firm, bronzed, muscular, drove everything else from her thoughts. She reached up for him and he lowered himself gently to her waiting arms.

She lost touch with time and space, felt herself spinning in a whirlpool of dizzying sensations. Together they explored new levels of awareness. Unable to resist the incredible passion that was stronger than anything she had felt before, she knew that although loving Colin had been a beautiful part of her life, it could never compare with the awesome bliss of Neil's lovemaking. Blood pulsed through her body. She lost herself in desire and plunged headlong into a spiral of melting, fiery bursts of ecstasy.

Long moments later, spent, they lay in each others' arms, and then she snuggled against his chest, sighed once more and drifted into peaceful sleep.

18

Ginger felt warmth steal across her body, then Neil's voice, as if coming from a great distance.

'Good morning, sweetheart.'

She turned and saw him outlined against the sunlight coming in the window. 'Good morning.'

Fully dressed, he bent to kiss her. 'You've been sleeping so soundly, I couldn't wake you, but I know your office opens when the New York Stock Exchange does.'

'What time is it?'

'Almost nine.'

She sat up quickly, instantly alert. 'Do you realize I'm three hours late for work?'

'I tried to wake you at six, but you turned over and went back to sleep again. I hope you won't be in trouble.'

Ginger sprang to her feet. 'No, it's

not that serious, and it's not your fault. I guess I needed all that sleep. You didn't happen to have a telephone installed in here yet, did you?'

'Yes, on the wall in the kitchen. I suppose it's working.'

'I'll call my office then and tell them I'm on my way.' She found one of the towels on the floor and wrapped it around her body, then followed him into the kitchen and made her call. He didn't make it easy for her, putting his arms around her waist, nuzzling her neck and kissing her ears.

When she hung up the telephone, she put her arms around his back and pressed him to her, savoring the hard muscles she could feel through his clothes. Letting go of her for a moment, he reached for the corner of the towel tucked under her left arm. She suspected his intention before he could act on the impulse, however, and in one deft moment she ducked away from him and retreated around the counter.

'Not so fast, my friend,' she laughed.

'You can't have the towel until you produce my clothes.'

'I don't know about you, but a cold shower this morning didn't diminish my desire for you one bit. If anything, it's stronger than before.' He moved slowly around the counter and soon stood close to her again.

She reveled in the words and the tone of his voice, but morning had come and duty called. 'Somehow I don't remember where I left my underwear.'

'Even if you remembered, you wouldn't have found it. I got up early this morning and found your things in the hot tub. I don't have a washer and dryer yet, so I had to dry them in the oven.' He opened the oven door and removed the garments. To her delight, Ginger found them warm and dry.

'Since you're late already,' he said, 'why don't we have some breakfast first? When I couldn't rouse you, I went up to the church and brought back some goodies.' He held up a paper plate with two large pastries. 'Actually I've

already eaten one, but being in love makes me hungry.' He grinned at her.

She couldn't help smiling back. Whether it was love or two days of hard work, something had given her an appetite as well.

'I've made hot coffee,' he continued, 'and I can warm these in the microwave.'

'You have a microwave oven?'

'Doesn't everyone? Do you?'

'Of course. It's the second best invention.'

'Second best? What's the first?

'Velcro.'

'Velcro? Who is he? I thought I was the only man in your life.' He came close and put his arms around her.

Between giggles, she said, 'Not being a woman, you wouldn't understand.'

'I think you're pulling my leg.'

'No, but that's an idea.' She stroked his thigh.

'I'll give you two hours to stop that.'

'Two hours?' Ginger came to her senses and backed away hurriedly. 'I

don't have two *minutes*. Can you save breakfast until after I shower?' She didn't wait for his answer, but spun around and dashed toward the master bathroom.

Guilt for her tardiness spurring her along, she made it her fastest shower on record. She put on her silk dress again, bundling up the clothes Denise Warshow had given her so she could return them to the church, then headed for the kitchen, her shoes in her hands.

The smell of fresh brewed coffee drew her like a magnet, and she crossed the dining room carpet soundlessly. Neil's back was to her: he spoke to someone on the telephone. Actually, he was murmuring, as if deliberately trying to be quiet, head down, shoulders hunched.

Even so, Ginger could hear his side of the conversation.

' — No one told me they'd do that this morning. But I think I should have been informed — I assume the tapes arrived — Saturday? Well, I didn't expect that — Yes, the investigation proceeded very smoothly, better than I thought. Mrs. Maddox doesn't know — Good. No, I have a lot of loose ends here — All right. Talk to you later.'

Ginger stood in the kitchen doorway, heart pounding, her throat tight. Neil replaced the receiver and stood still, staring at the telephone as if deep in thought. She dropped her shoes and they clattered loudly on the kitchen floor.

'Ginger!' He whirled around, surprise and dismay written on his face.

'You — you — ' Words refused to form at first, and she stood still, fists clenched at her sides, her breath beginning to come in short gasps. 'I trusted you, and you — '

'Ginger, what did you hear?'

'I heard it all! You've been investigating me! Time after time I had suspicions and you always managed to lie your way out of them — '

'I never lied to you.' He moved toward her, but she stopped him with a look.

'This has all been a masquerade. First came the mysterious business about Harlan Taylor, but you had an answer for that. You were his friend. Then the man in the park. You said he asked you for directions, but you knew him, didn't you? Who was he, another spy? Was he following me too, just in case you missed something?'

She knew her voice was rising, getting shrill, but she didn't care. She wanted to do more than shout; she wanted to scream, to throw things at him, to claw at his face with her nails. How dare he do this to her?

'Ginger, you're not listening to me.'

'Oh, I listened to you before. Last night you put on another mask. You played the part of a lover, telling me you loved me, and, like a fool, I believed you. When all the time you were spying on me!'

'No — '

'You pretended to care for me, but instead you were only investigating.' The last words were almost a shriek.

'Ginger, you must calm down and let me explain.'

Breasts heaving, she realized she could hardly breathe. 'Go ahead, start explaining again. That'll be a laugh!'

'First I have to call New York again. I'm not even sure I can tell you anything.'

'Oh, that's a good one,' she said sarcastically. 'That's very good.'

'You have to believe me; I would never hurt you.'

'Just answer one question. The truth, Neil, make it the truth just this once.'

'Anything.'

'Were you investigating me?'

His eyes bored into hers and the golden brown color changed to deep black. Pain etched lines down his cheeks and set his jaw into a hard ridge.

Seconds passed before the muffled word finally emerged. 'Yes.'

Ginger thought she would faint. He could have lied, but instead he told the truth. Somehow that was even harder to bear. She forced the words from her throat. 'That's all I need to hear.'

She turned and left the kitchen, but he followed and stopped her when she got to the front hallway.

'But it's not what you think,' he said. 'I did investigate you. I had to. But later I realized you weren't involved.'

'You pretended. It was all a masquerade.'

'I never pretended with you, Ginger. I fell in love with you right from the start. I love you now.'

'Lying comes easily to you. That's part of your job, isn't it? You're a detective.'

'I used to be.'

'And then you quit when you went to New York. Don't bother telling me that lie again. I remember it from before.'

Suddenly the doorbell rang loudly, its chimes echoing against the empty walls. Neil gave her a pleading look, then crossed to the front door and opened it. A uniformed man stood there, his truck, the side reading, 'Bay Area Catering.' stood at the curb.

'I'm here for a pick-up,' the young man said. 'Hey, you guys had some earthquake, didn't you? I was surprised I could even get up here today.'

Neil cut him short, pointing. 'The containers are in the kitchen.'

The young man shrugged and came inside.

Thoughts racing, Ginger spoke to him. 'Are you going back to the city? Will you take me with you?'

He looked puzzled, seemed about to say 'no,' then apparently changed his mind. 'Sure, Lady, I can drop you downtown.'

She followed him to the kitchen. Her shoes still lay in the doorway and she slipped them on. Then, while he carried the containers, she hurried toward his truck.

Neil came up behind her, his voice tense. 'Ginger, don't do this to us. I can explain, believe me. I just need a little time. I'm not in this alone, you know. I have to obey orders.'

'I have nothing to say to you, and

there's nothing you could possibly say to me.' Amazingly, her voice sounded calm, but her heart felt as if it were being torn in two.

Her eyes burned with unshed tears, but after she climbed into the seat next to the driver, and he pulled away down the hill, she let them come. They ran down her face silently, making salty pools at the corners of her mouth.

19

Ginger rode back to the city under a brilliant blue sky, the sun dazzlingly bright. For once, the sight held no pleasure for her, instead her tears flowed even faster. The mood established over the weekend was irrevocably broken. He said he loved her and they had consummated their love. But now the reality of his mysterious past and his confession had plunged her into depths of pain and despair that no amount of sunshine could reach.

The driver of the catering truck respected her mood and didn't speak. Finally she gained control of her emotions and dried her tears. 'Thanks for the lift,' she said. 'Sorry about my behavior, but it's been a rough morning.'

'I understand,' he said. 'Like the song says, breaking up is tough.' After a short pause, he added, 'You want some coffee? I got some in that thermos next to you and there's cups in that plastic bag.'

Ginger picked up the thermos, unscrewed the top and poured coffee into one of the Styrofoam cups. Remembering that she had never gotten around to the coffee and a pastry Neil had waiting for her in his kitchen almost brought on a fresh bout of tears, but she took a deep breath and forced herself to respond to the driver's comments about the earthquake.

'It was a six-point-seven,' he said, 'pretty strong.'

'Yes, some houses were damaged and trees uprooted.' She told him how the trees in the road had prevented them from leaving the area and how the local church had helped everyone, without mentioning her own role in the process.

Sooner than she expected, he dropped her at her apartment, where she paused only long enough to change into a clean suit, then hopped a cable car to go to her office. With trembling fingers she unfolded the *Wall Street Journal* on her desk.

On page one, an article about First Continental leaped out at her: after the stock dropped another five points on Friday, the Securities and Exchange Commission considered investigating irregularities in trading, suspecting insider manipulation. She read on with steadily mounting pulse, trying to sort out what it meant to her and to her clients. Almost automatically, she punched the keys of the terminal to get a quote, and the words flashed at her. 'Trading suspended.' No one could buy or sell shares in the stock until the ban was lifted.

Her thoughts centered on the Dillon sisters. They'd been selling short right up to the end, and had covered on Friday, making a very tidy profit. How convenient. How lucky. Did they somehow have insider information? If so, where did they get it? Neil's face floated before her eyes. Of course. He gave it to them.

First there had been Taylor Technology. He had known the takeover attempt wouldn't succeed. How could he know that, unless he had access to illegal information? She'd asked him those questions before and he covered by saying it was not really a takeover but someone selling confidential information. But now, everything had changed. Her doubts returned stronger than ever. Perhaps Harlan Taylor himself had given information to Neil. They had been college friends, after all. And although Neil told her he had never been to San Francisco until then, that didn't necessarily make it so. Men had lied to women before. Even women they said they cared deeply for. Or, perhaps especially those.

The churnings in her stomach became unbearable and Ginger rested her face in the palms of her hands. She was deeply in love with Neil; at least she'd been certain of that last night. But his revelation made it clear he was involved in something illegal. Where could she turn?

She would ask Jim Blake. At once she rejected that thought. In the first place, it would be too humiliating to admit a man she'd slept with might be some kind of criminal. Second, she had no proof of anything. She had overheard a telephone conversation, accused him of spying on her, which he admitted. Nothing more. Perhaps she should have stayed, questioned him, got the facts. But his betrayal drove everything else from her head. She could hardly bear to think that after finally allowing herself to love again she'd chosen a man guaranteed to bring her nothing but pain and anguish.

Her telephone rang and, pushing her thoughts aside, she took the call. When she finished answering her client's questions, she turned again to her dilemma over Neil.

What about the newsletter he worked for, 'Good Times,' and its owner Ned

Weiser? She would call him and find out just how much he knew about Neil Cameron. But no one answered the telephone when she called the number Neil had given her.

'Ginger.' Neil came into her cubicle and dropped into the opposite chair.

Shock made her knees weak and her stomach tighten. 'How dare you come here?' she said between clenched teeth, fighting to keep her voice low.

'I need to talk to you.' He wore a tan business suit, shirt and tie, looked as handsome as ever, but pale.

'About what? Surely it couldn't be about First Continental stock?'

'Then you've heard?'

'I'm probably the last broker in San Francisco to have learned it. thanks to you, but, yes, I heard.'

'I'll explain everything if you'll just listen.'

'About your involvement? You are involved in it, aren't you? Or is it about your aunts' selling, about your passing insider information to them?'

'My aunts' selling? What do you mean?'

'I mean they were short-selling the stock. Don't pretend you didn't know. Obviously, you put them up to it. They closed out their position Friday.' She almost shouted the last word. 'How else could they know it would happen?'

'They were short-selling? That's ridiculous!'

'I wasn't to tell you,' Ginger said. 'They swore me to secrecy. What a fool I've been!'

'Ginger, please believe me when I say I knew nothing about that. When I questioned you about your recommendations to my aunts and you told me to ask them, I did just that. But they refused to tell me. They said I should mind my own business. I had no idea they were involved in First Continental.'

'How can I believe anything you say? You were spying on me, making love to me to keep me from suspecting the truth.' Saying the words aloud brought fresh bursts of pain, and she closed her eyes tightly.

'Just what do you think the truth is? What do you hold me responsible for?'

Ginger had been unable to answer that question herself. In some ways nothing made sense. Slowly, she put her fears into words, spoke carefully and kept her voice under control. 'You had insider information about First Continental and you passed it on to a lot of people, not just your aunts.'

'Why would I do that?'

'For money, of course.'

'That's not so.'

'There's still Taylor Technology.'

'I've already explained that.'

'First you said there was to be a takeover, then you changed it to insider fraud, and now the same thing is happening at First Continental. And you were involved in both of them.' He couldn't deny it in the face of all the evidence.

Before he could answer, her telephone rang, and Ginger picked it up.

She did more listening than speaking, making notes, and finally hung up.

'Wait a minute,' Neil said. 'I can clear up everything if you'll just let me explain.'

Once more the telephone interrupted them and Ginger handled the call before again looking up at Neil.

'Ginger, you can't have it both ways. If I had all this insider information, why would I need to spy on you? You certainly didn't pass any on to me.'

'You wanted to be sure I hadn't caught on — '

His bitter laugh interrupted her. 'I should have told you at the time, but I couldn't take a chance. I have nothing to reproach myself for unless it's falling in love with you.'

Ginger's heart plummeted and she couldn't speak. Did he regret everything he'd said? But surely, she played the bigger fool, for having allowed herself to do the same, when she still had so many doubts. Now *he* pretended to be the victim. Her anger returned.

'Since you're used to lying, I'm sure you can clear your conscience quickly.'

His face changed. Lines creased his forehead and appeared at the corners of his mouth. 'Apparently our weekend together didn't mean as much to you as it did to me.'

'I think that's obvious. I thought we were having a love affair. Instead you used me. I was never anything more to you than a 'case.''

The telephone jangled at her side.

'Dammit,' Neil exploded, 'I'd stand a better chance of talking to you if I went to a phone booth! I'll come by your apartment tonight and explain everything.'

'I don't recall inviting you to my apartment.' Her hurt made her eyes burn and her vision blur.

He'd been on his feet for some seconds and then he leaned forward across the desk, and stared into her eyes. 'Don't do this, Ginger. I can be just as stubborn as you can, you know. I have the red hair to prove it!'

Reason had long since flown. She wanted only to lash out at him, to punish him for the despair that consumed her insides.

'If you show up, I'll call the police and have you arrested. I should probably do that anyway. The article says the S.E.C. is investigating. Well, I for one, will see they investigate you!'

'For the last time, will you hold your phone calls for five minutes and let me explain to you?' Desperation edged his voice.

'No!'

With that he turned and strode from the office, leaving Ginger with fire burning in her throat. She would have her revenge at least. She dialed the number of the Securities and Exchange Commission. 'I'm calling about the First Continental investigation and a Mr. Neil Cameron.'

'One moment, please.'

Eventually a masculine voice came on the line. 'Mr. Cameron is busy with that investigation and not available. Can I help you?'

* * *

The rest of the day seemed endless. It ought to have gone quickly, because her phone never seemed to stop ringing, and she handled three times as many transactions as normal, to say nothing of having to explain to those of her customers who still owned First Continental what the suspension in trading might mean to their accounts.

Finally every buy and sell order, every pink telephone message, had been disposed of, and she realized the office had become very quiet. She rose and arched her back, feeling the tense muscles across her shoulders and noticing that only one other representative was still at his desk, head bowed in concentration. She retrieved her purse, walked silently through the large outer office and out the glass doors onto Montgomery Street. The air was warmer than usual and no fog hung over the tops of the skyscrapers that afternoon. She pulled off her suit jacket and carried it over her arm while she walked to the cable car that would take her back to her apartment.

Once inside, she undressed, hung up her street clothes and slipped into shorts and a tee shirt. Being on the top floor, her apartment had trapped the uncommon heat of the day, and she felt uncomfortably warm already. In addition, the dull ache that had begun the moment she learned that Neil had been employed by the S.E.C. would not go away. She tried to push her agony to the back of her mind. She had to face it; she'd been too hasty to judge, had said things that now made her cringe.

Barefoot, she went into the kitchen and opened her refrigerator, but nothing appealed to her. She thought of all the cooking she'd done all weekend, of eating all her meals with Neil.

No, she would not think about him. Fighting down anger and regret, she heated a can of soup but, after one spoonful, realized her queasy stomach wouldn't let her eat. She went into the living room, where she plopped down on the window seat and let herself give way to weeping. What a fool she was. She'd been given another chance for love, and had thrown it away in her usual impetuous fashion. Neil had done his best to answer her questions, and she had insisted on doubting him. Worse, she had refused even to let him explain.

The tree which grew just under the window was in full leaf, somewhat shading the window from the sun. She leaned back against the casement and her silent tears gave way to wracking sobs. Finally, her crying stopped, but she felt exhausted, not only from the heat but from the turmoil in her thoughts. She got up and went to the wing chair, then saw the small stuffed bear Neil had won for her at the carnival on the Fourth of July. She untied the silk scarf from around its neck and put it on her own. Neil had said that if he were a knight in a joust, the scarf would show that she was his lady fair. But she had spoiled her chance and it was too late now to admit she would give anything to be Neil's lady.

20

Ginger wakened at her usual early hour the next day, although she'd fallen asleep lying across her bed still wearing her shorts, tee shirt and the silk scarf Neil had given her. She dressed in her pink linen suit, but instead of wearing the blouse that went with it, she again tied the silk scarf at her neck. Then she rode the cable car to her office.

Her first call was from Mary Dillon, asking her to come to the Greenhouse Restaurant for lunch. Ginger readily agreed; she had a dozen questions for the ladies. But after she asked the hostess for the Dillon sisters' table, she was taken to an empty booth. Neil's two aunts had not yet arrived. It wasn't like them to be late, but she only shrugged, sat down and picked up the menu. Then, a tall figure came up swiftly and sat next to her. Neil.

His eyes were bloodshot, his jaw firm and hard, but his gaze fell on the scarf at her throat, and his voice softened. 'Don't get up. My aunts aren't coming. I'm sorry about the deception but I had to see you and I asked them to arrange it this way.'

She had no intention of leaving. His appearance was an answer to her prayers. She wanted to apologize but didn't know how to start.

'Ginger, we can't have misunderstandings between us like this. When I left you yesterday, I called New York and got permission to tell you what's been going on.'

'I called New York, too. I know that you work for the Securities and Exchange Commission. Oh, Neil, I'm so ashamed for everything I said and did yesterday.'

His eyes widened and then he slid closer to her in the booth, and took both her hands in his. 'My fault. I should have told you all about it long ago.'

'You tried but I wouldn't let you. I was so angry.'

He leaned closer and kissed her quickly, tenderly. 'Ginger, I've been in agony since yesterday. I've been trying to reassure myself that I haven't actually lied to you, but the fact is, I certainly never told you the whole truth.'

The whole truth? Was there more? She didn't want to hear anything that might threaten their love again. 'You don't have to tell me — ' she began.

'And not just today. So many times in these past weeks I've felt guilty about keeping you in the dark.'

'Sometimes,' she said, remembering, 'you'd look at me so strangely.'

'Thank God it's behind us now.' He took a deep breath. 'Here's the story. I've worked for the S.E.C. for about five years. A few months ago, wanting to make a change, I looked around for something else. That's when Harlan Taylor called me.'

'Then there is a connection between

313

Harlan Taylor and First Continental?'

'Yes, there is a link, which I'll get to in a minute. This is a long story, but I'll try to keep it uncomplicated. First, a couple of months ago, Harlan called me from California and said he thought some unethical practices were going on in his company. Knowing I worked for the S.E.C., he asked about unfriendly takeovers and I told him what I knew. He didn't want us to investigate, but apparently I gave him enough that he at least knew what to look for. He ousted one of the officers of his company, someone who stood to make a lot of money at Harlan's — and the company's — expense.'

'Carl Rivvio, who resigned.'

'Yes, but that's not all.'

'Go on.'

A waitress came by to take their order, but Neil waved her away. 'When he called to tell me he finally had it under control, he mentioned the name of a man who had been working with his unscrupulous officer. The man's

314

name was Ned Weiser.'

'Your Ned Weiser?' Ginger said.

'The same. But I didn't work with him then, not 'till I offered to be a writer for his newsletter.'

'But why did you go to work for him if you knew he'd been involved in the problem at Taylor Technology?'

'To investigate any further illegal activities. I wanted to put him out of business for good.'

'For the S.E.C.?'

'Yes and no. I was in the midst of resigning by then. I took the job with Weiser and immediately learned that he had an associate here on the West Coast who made a lot of contacts for him. I suspected he was the middle man between Weiser and Taylor Technology. If I could find proof of the leak, I could keep it from happening again. That was the person I had to find. And I did. His next target was First Continental. He would buy insider information and pass it through Weiser.'

'Printing it in his newsletter?'

'No, selling it to certain wealthy subscribers as a special service. Probably they didn't suspect he obtained it illegally, but the S.E.C. will determine that. Lots of money can be made by anticipating dips and rises in the price of stocks.'

Ginger didn't interrupt but kept holding his hand.

'So I pretended ignorance, told Weiser I wanted to open an office out here and came out to find the man who was buying the insider information. Then I played the part of an investor looking for a hot tip and persuaded him to tell me how the scam worked. Last Friday, I mailed a list of names and a tape recording of my conversation with him, along with the tape of a later telephone call to Weiser, to the S.E.C.'

Things were making sense at last. 'So that explains why you had a tape recorder in your bag at the Fourth of July festival.'

'How did you know about that?'

'I saw it there when you went to get our dinner.'

'We made an appointment to meet that day and he contacted me while you were changing clothes.'

'I saw you together when I came out, and you had your hand inside the bag. It looked odd. The man looked so strange, I wondered what you were doing.'

'You must have been very puzzled.'

'Yes. Later I thought you were taping me. You even admitted it yesterday.'

'I never taped any of our conversations, and I investigated you very briefly. Thanks to my years as a detective, I learned that your husband, Colin, had been the broker for Rivvio. I had to find out if he, or you, were profiting from insider information too.'

'That explains all those questions about my attitude toward money.' She looked into his eyes for confirmation.

'I exonerated you long before that. I learned right away that everything was above-board there. No, my sweet, I began investigating you for my own purposes.' He paused and looked as if he wanted to kiss her again, but instead rushed on, finishing his explanations. 'I sent the tapes on Friday, expecting them to arrive today, but they actually got there Saturday.'

'And the S.E.C. suspended trading in the stock,' she finished. 'Will that straighten it all out and put the guilty people in jail?'

He shrugged. 'Something like that. I'm sorry I couldn't tell you all about it before, but it had to be done in secret.'

'Just as I was sworn to secrecy by your aunts.'

'Yes. I still don't know how they happened to sell the stock short. Must have been a coincidence. I think they sometimes use tarot cards and fortune-telling to get their tips. Who knows where they got that one?'

'Well, they didn't do anything illegal, did they?'

'No. I checked that out yesterday,

after you told me about their short-selling. Their names were never mentioned in this deal. They don't know any of the officers or insiders of the company. As I said, it can only have been a coincidence, just as any investor might have bought or sold stock in the company.' He looked at her quizzically. 'You had several customers for the stock yourself, didn't you?'

'Not many were left, although I certainly never suggested that anyone sell short.'

'It's not a bad technique, especially if you know in advance what's going to happen, like Ned Weiser did.'

'And he told you.'

'Yes, but I didn't take advantage of it.'

'You could have made a lot of money,' Ginger said.

'S.E.C. employees are under very strict rules about investing. That's one of the reasons I decided to resign.'

'And you don't have a job with Weiser anymore.'

'No, I seem to be currently unemployed.' His eyes twinkled with humor. 'Is that all right with you?'

'Anything you do is all right with me as long as you don't go away. You don't have to go back to New York, do you?'

'No, I'd never do that, unless you came with me. I'll find something out here.'

'I'll support both of us for a while, if necessary.' The words seemed to leap out as if of their own accord and Ginger let go of his hand and took a sip of water to cover her sudden nervousness. 'That is, if you still love me.'

'You know I do.'

'I'll never forgive myself for the way I behaved yesterday morning. But I hurt so much. I guess until then I hadn't let myself admit I could care this much for anyone.'

'Are you used to the idea now?'

'Yes.' She leaned against him and he put one hand around her back. 'Neil — '

'Yes, love.'

'I don't have to go back to the office until tomorrow morning. Can we spend the whole afternoon together?'

'And the evening,' he added, pressing her closer.

'Ahem.' It was the waitress again, and this time Neil didn't shoo her away.

'What do you want?' he asked, scanning the menu.

'You order for me,' Ginger said, not bothering to open hers. 'Just remember, I'm famished.'

When the waitress left, Neil again reached for Ginger's hands and squeezed them. 'Being in love agrees with you. You have a healthy appetite, and you glow like a star. From the first moment I saw you, I thought you were the most beautiful woman I'd seen in San Francisco, but now I'm sure it's the world.'

'Stop! You'll make me blush.'

'You'll make a radiant bride.'

Ginger felt her happy grin dissolve into a serious look. The excitement of being in love, of having Neil love her in

321

return, was suddenly overwhelmed by his words.

'Will you marry me, Ginger? I know I don't have a regular job but I supported myself for years with investments.'

For a long moment she couldn't answer. Her moment of truth had come. Yet, no ambivalence clouded her judgment. She knew she was ready for this step, that she had been for several days. She would always cherish the beautiful memory of Colin, but Neil was the future, an exciting future. 'Yes,' she said, her voice a choked whisper. 'Oh, yes,' she said, more loudly.

'Hooray!' The two feminine voices that had made the exclamation came from behind Ginger.

She whirled around and saw two identical grins on the faces of Neil's two aunts, who were seated beyond an enormous palm tree. Again she was speechless.

'Congratulations,' Mary Dillon said to her nephew, and the ladies pulled their chairs away from the protective cover of the shrubbery. 'We knew you could do it.'

'And you must get married right away,' Carrie Dillon added, 'because we're not getting any younger, you know, and we want to see lots of red-headed great-nieces and nephews.'

'Miss Dillon — ' Ginger began.

'Aunt Mary,' Mary Dillon corrected. 'We're going to be related now.'

'Aunt Mary, you two have been spying on us, haven't you?' Neil asked, pretending to be annoyed.

'No, of course not,' Carrie answered through a grin.

'We lunch here often,' Mary added. 'But I will admit,' she giggled behind one hand, 'when we arranged for you to be here — '

' — we asked for a table nearby,' Carrie finished.

'And now that you've found out,' Neil continued, 'I want to remind you of something else you've done recently — '

'Do you mean our selling short in

First Continental stock?'

' — and getting out again just before they stopped trading?' Carrie added, then turned to her sister. 'My, we had precise timing, didn't we? Even we didn't think we'd be *that* good!'

'Just where did you get that stock tip to short-sell First Continental, from a fortune teller?' Neil asked.

'Why, of course not. You don't really think we get stock market suggestions from that kind of thing, do you?' She sounded shocked that anyone would suspect them of such ridiculous behavior.

'No, we got it from our book, of course. You remember, my dear,' Mary turned to Ginger for confirmation, 'we told you we had read the most remarkable book about stock market timing.'

'I remember.' She had to turn her head from side to side again, as the ladies alternated speaking.

'Well, Carrie continued, 'that book told us about cycles, and we could see that First Continental had a down cycle so we were supposed to sell short.'

'We've never done that before,' Mary added, 'but it was a lot of fun.'

'And very dangerous,' Neil reminded them. 'You could have lost a lot of money.'

'I don't think so,' Carrie commented confidently. 'If you follow the rules — '

'But you didn't know someone deliberately manipulated the stock. If you had delayed from Friday to Monday, you'd be in a much different position today.'

'That was lucky,' Mary admitted, 'still, the rules — '

'I can't contradict that.' Neil shrugged and shook his head. 'It's very hard to argue with success. But do be more careful in the future. Let Ginger suggest stocks to you.'

'Oh, we admit Ginger's very good — ' Mary said.

'But the fact is,' Ginger said, 'you never asked me for a single stock suggestion. You've done very well without me. Perhaps I should take advice from you.'

They all laughed, and then Ginger turned to Carrie Dillon again. 'There is one thing I want to know. Why did you wait so long to contact me? When my husband died, you didn't move your account or even do any trading until Neil came to San Francisco.'

'Well, my dear, we don't use fortune telling, but we do have a very dear friend who's a psychic and she saw — mentally you understand — the accident in which your husband was killed. She told us that someone else would come who would be important in our lives, and we were to wait. Then Neil called us and said he had met you, and when we asked our friend, she said you were the person we were waiting for.' She smiled a very smug, self-satisfied smile, then looked puzzled and apologetic and, turning to her sister, said, 'Oh, dear, I seem to have made a speech!'

Neil took his aunts' hands in his for a

moment, then released them and touched Ginger's cheeks in a tender gesture that told her how much he loved her. 'You were only partly right. Ginger is the person *I* was waiting for!'

THE END

We do hope that you have enjoyed reading this large print book.

Did you know that all of our titles are available for purchase?

We publish a wide range of high quality large print books including:
Romances, Mysteries, Classics
General Fiction
Non Fiction and Westerns

Special interest titles available in large print are:
The Little Oxford Dictionary
Music Book, Song Book
Hymn Book, Service Book

Also available from us courtesy of Oxford University Press:
Young Readers' Dictionary
(large print edition)
Young Readers' Thesaurus
(large print edition)

For further information or a free brochure, please contact us at:
Ulverscroft Large Print Books Ltd.,
The Green, Bradgate Road, Anstey,
Leicester, LE7 7FU, England.
Tel: (00 44) **0116 236 4325**
Fax: (00 44) **0116 234 0205**

ELUSIVE LOVE

Karen Abbott

Amelia has always been determined to marry for love . . . but with her elder brother dead and posthumously branded as a traitor, Amelia and her sister find themselves penniless and ostracised by society. When a relative contrives to put an *'eligible parti'* under an obligation to make Amelia an offer, Amelia has to decide whether or not to stand by her principles . . . and face the consequences of turning down what might be her only chance to escape her unbearable situation.

MARRIED TO THE ENEMY

Sheila Holroyd

Faced with the choice of death or marriage to a stranger, Kate marries Lord Alvedon, the powerful servant of Queen Elizabeth. Taken away from everything she has ever known Kate finds it difficult to adjust to the strange new world of Elizabeth's court. Her innocence not only threatens her marriage, it puts her in great danger — and, unknown to her or her husband, a secret enemy plans to kill both of them . . .

TABITHA'S TRIALS

Valerie Holmes

Tabitha is reluctantly released from St Mary's Establishment for Impoverished Girls because Miss Grimley will not break the rules and allow her to remain. She must go into service, contributing to the school so that other girls will benefit. Tabitha rides on the back of a wagon and watches her past drift into the distance. With a heavy heart, she contemplates years of hard work and predictability stretching before her, little realising just what the future has to offer . . .

GENTLEMEN PREFER . . . BRUNETTES

Liz Fielding

Nick Jefferson can't resist a challenge, or a blonde! So when the latest platinum-haired woman to cross his path challenges him to cook her a romantic dinner, he accepts. Unfortunately Nick could burn water . . . Chef Cassie Cornwell is *not* Nick's type — she's a brunette, and the only woman to turn Nick down. She's disappointed he wants her to prepare a seduction feast rather than to share one. Unless Cassie can persuade him that blondes aren't necessarily more fun . . .

THE HONEY TREE

Glenis Wilson

Sparks fly when Merri Williams meets Walt Lime. She's struggling to keep Aunt Prue's riding stables afloat whilst Prue and Walt's Uncle Matt are in Dubai. To avoid bankruptcy, Merri buys more ponies and gives riding lessons to disabled children. But Walt is intent on stopping her. What is he concealing? And why has Prue gone to Dubai? 'When I return I'll tell you — until then you'll be on your own — promise you'll ask Walt for help . . . '

A SUBTLE DECEIT

Anne Hewland

Two eligible gentlemen bring Nerissa Cleveland news of her father's death in Egypt — the unassuming Bernard Martin and the darkly abrupt Lord Brook. Both offer to help her to deal with Giles Cleveland's collection of antiquities — which now seems to be at risk from intruders. The neglected house and grounds hold many secrets ... but who will assist Nerissa in unravelling the mysteries? Does one of her suitors have sinister motives ... ? And who will gain her love?